More Praise for Stacey Levine...

Amid alarming depictions of domestic misery and perversion, strange metamorphoses, and imperiled nature, as well as the occasional triumphant escape or alliance, Levine declares the death of myth and anticipates the collapse of civilization. But for now, she subtly acknowledges that however deluded, poisoned, and impaired we may be, we will continue to tell and cherish tales and stories as we struggle against lies, brutality, and alienation.

      Donna Seaman, *Bookforum*

Levine's crisp stories similarly find excitement and transformation as they chase down their fantastical plots. *The Girl with Brown Fur* won't be everyone's cup of tea, but the adventurous will enjoy following Levine's bread-crumb trails, even if that means getting a little bit lost.

      A.N. Devers, *Time Out New York*

Reading *The Girl with Brown Fur: Tales and Stories* is like exploring a city not your own in a robot submarine. Prepare for Stacey Levine's sentences or they will eat you. Take time off work, call in sick, give yourself a week. Like all good vacations, it's easy to move from weddings to wolves to sausages so quickly that all significance is lost, coalescing into one massive beast in your tinny mind—all because you're in rush. Slow down. Make soup. Kidnap sal bugs. Each tale requires its own moment.

      William Gallien, *Alice Blue Review*

How might one become complete? A fulfilled human being? Own a cat and as it ages, clone it. Fly your airplane away from your mother's illness. Produce an extraordinary amount of sausage. Marry the first woman who walks into your place of business, and if she runs off to Ohio, take her to Rome. Steal an enslaved girl covered in whitish-brown fur. The inhabitants of Stacey Levine's stories attempt each of these things and more, with no more success than people who have extramarital affairs or people who buy sports cars. Thankfully, Levine's stories have a refreshing lack of respect for reality.

Nick Bredie, *The Believer*

A few words about Stacey Levine: Brilliant. Surprising. Unsettling. One of a kind.

Jonathan Evison, author of *West of Here* and *All About Lulu*

On Levine's novel *Frances Johnson...*

Levine's work is, at least technically, "surreal," but like much of the best writing that maps the borders between dreams and conscious life, its subtle disjunctions create a zone that often feels more real than "reality" itself.... If it feels like we've been here before, underneath this dance floor, gazing up at the townsfolk above, it is not because we've seen this landscape in other fictions, but maybe in a half-remembered dream.

Stephen Beachy, *San Francisco Bay Guardian*

What makes the book compelling, much like Levine's debut novel, *Dra—*, is its play of words and images, its irregular pacing and its capture of what it means to be trapped in a life with meaningless choices. Frances spends a night with a man who lives in a cave, discovers a scar on her leg that may or may not be a tumor and kisses her boyfriend's brother for no apparent reason and to no apparent consequence. Each vignette has a strange, almost possible quality. "For how long will Frances Johnson go in circles?" the omniscient narrator asks rhetorically at one point. Readers of this pocket-sized book will indulge her as long as she likes.

Publisher's Weekly

This is a comedy of manners, and there is an inkling of Austen in Levine's delicate and deadpan assault on our culture's heterosexist, heterogeneous dictates. But the feel of the novel is more fanciful than programmatic. Each sentence operates in the same manner as the overarching narrative: shifting shape, defying expectation.

Jason McBride, *The Believer*

There are dreams in every living mind, blood squeezed and sucked by vessels in every body, and people can also be damned annoying, sneaking up behind you and trying to kiss you in parking lots. It is a pleasure to find new novels that regard and represent real life in such full, evasive circumferences.

Rain Taxi Review of Books

THE GIRL WITH BROWN FUR

Stacey Levine

tales and stories

Starcherone Books   Buffalo, NY

These stories appeared in the following venues:
"Uppsala" in *Snow Flake*; "The Bean" in *The Stranger, Waterstone,* and in a shorter form as a comic with illustrations by Renee French in *Marbles in My Underpants: The Renee French Collection*; "The Girl" in *Tin House*; "The Wolf" in *Seattle Magazine*; "Alia" in *Tantalum,* and originally as "Bird-Smitten Uncle" in *The Stranger*; "Milk Boy" in *Yeti*; "Sausage" in *The Iowa Review*; "Lax Forb" in *the Denver Quarterly*; "Pat Smash" in *3rd Bed*; "The Cat" in *Denver Quarterly*; "The Kidney Problem" in *Fence*; "Scoo Boy" in *The Washington Review*; "The World of Barry" in *Notre Dame Review*; "The Fields" in *Northwest Edge III*; "The Tree" in *The Fairy Tale Review*; "Ears" in *Golden Handcuffs Review*; and "The Water" in *The New Review of Literature.*

Editor: Ted Pelton
Book Designer: Rebecca Maslen
Cover Art: "The Girl with Brown Fur" by Tae Won Yu
Proofreaders: Thomas McGrath and Jason Pontillo

Library of Congress Cataloging-in-Publication Data

Levine, Stacey.
 The girl with brown fur : tales & stories / Stacey Levine.
    p. cm.
   Summary: "A collection of short stories by Stacey Levine, an author known for her use of strange disjunctions, odd plots, quirky characters, and surreal elements, as well as for her meticulous language"-- Provided by publisher.
 ISBN 978-0-9842133-4-4 (pbk.)
 I. Title.
 PS3562.E912G57 2011
 813'.54--dc22
                              2010053896

Acknowledgements:

To Artist Trust of Seattle, for support.

To Seattle's Richard Hugo House, for support. "The Danas" was commissioned by Hugo House as part of its 2007 "Telling Childhood" literary series.

To the Frye Art Museum of Seattle, WA, which commissioned "The Cats" as a response to sculpture by Patricia Piccinini in its New Works Reading Performance. Grateful thanks to the Frye for its exceptional attention in fostering creative work.

To Matthew Stadler and Publication Studio of Portland, OR, for vision and dedication in getting books to readers. This collection was available from PS in 2009-2010.

A Special Thank-You: Bill Abelson, Lisa Albers, Yasmine Alwan, Shannon Borg, Rebecca Brown, Lyall Bush, Sheri Cohen, Steve Connell, Jeffrey DeShell, Anna Maria Hong, Rich Jensen, Glenn MacGilvra, Paul Maliszewski, Douglas Messerli, Bill Miller, Lee Montgomery, Elizabeth Rieman, Dan Savage, Vince Standley, Lynne Tillman, Benjamin Weissman, Khristina Wenzinger, Emily White, Susan Willmarth, Deborah Woodard, Asher Wycoff, Corrina Wycoff, Diane Zerbe.

Table of Contents

Uppsala

We come from a bad family and we are disgraced.

"What time do we get there?" asks Brother.

"Stop cluttering your mind with those kinds of thoughts," answers Mother. It is Brother's nineteenth birthday, and we are driving off to the cabin.

We think she is terrible.

The true source of our family remains unknown, though it effectively has prevented speech and compassion for the speechless.

Destination: our vacation home in Uppsala.

The mountains luminously shore up the family cabin and our cheeks burn red. In our tiny battered car, we make bare progress along the road with its columnar, trembling snow.

Amidst the piercing whiteness of which exist our wishes that combine to produce friction of desperate severity.

Where is the family we know?

Here, only here.

My brother speaks his own language, he always did, sitting behind a TV tray, or silently loading an ebony water pistol with saliva toward the purpose of expressing both his inborn glee and the necessity of being inarticulate around Mother. Father resembles a hassock.

Suddenly, of an evening, an angry, upset scream from within the cabin. It is Mother, who saw a flea, and fleas are a sign of dirt. Soon after, another unbearable scream. She has forgotten to bring along a loaf of bread. Such occurrences are irreparable to her; she cannot contain her fear though thankfully the snow has already fallen, the cold loam that quiets all sound and sharpens our sight.

Brother has spit up on the floor, rolling in it, kicking his hard shoes upon the newspaper. The headlines of which describe a recent outstanding economic boom. Father, perhaps reading, perhaps not, blinks. The roof is stupendously heavy.

Our nights are static and lonely as ice gathers around the perimeter of this family kitchen, this apothecary, this place in which even weak, leftover tea is as potent as methanol.

"Sonofabitch!" Mother screams maniacally from the rear bedroom, for she has misplaced her pendant.

Brother utters a chain of rough syllables into my hair.

If she is terrible, we say, the source of her anguish is a world beyond ours which we do not know, but which we can read like a stencil around her obfuscating yells and lies.

Is the cold northern angel a mere provocateur aiming to stir Brother and me to desire something, anything, in the way of solace and succulence?

Our family is sad and does not live in a verdant place.

Distant snowaceous drifts, silhouettes of snow-burdened trees. The mountains which are ticking. We remain indoors, and the little valley below our cabin is ceaselessly untouched.

Brother and I have an interview in the toilet. We must have it in us to relax—surely this is our atavistic right? But we are bound in a community tension and a stupendous threat the name of which only Mother knows. Unfortunately, there are no witnesses to this conundrum aside from the breeze which shoots from the table of snow. Perhaps the mountain itself.

The deep snow there which has intercepted our wills with its radar and produced in us a wish to raze the ideas upon which the world is founded.

Brother and I have known only Sweden.

He has comforted me with the unspeakably thin parchment of his chest. Because of our wounds, we each have grown permeable and have for example consoled one another at twilight. He babbles incurably gentle, ambiguous words that seal our complicity, and this is love to which nothing else dares compare.

A ruffled curtain of snow floating in the sky at dawn disguises all glare. Laughter and screams from the kitchen. We wish to flee, draw the weight of the weather to our breasts, interpolate the valley with our tired knowledge, never be alone.

Beside me in the bathroom, Brother seems to say that we must reason with our family, try to talk. I am stunned; I violently disagree. We begin to struggle, grunting and slapping, bruising one another on the floor. Snow crusts drop from the window outside. Father hears, approaching with his hesitant curiosity. Then, the resoundingly loud footsteps of Mother.

That winter we learned the snow incited our games and the desire to freeze away our mother's sickness and we grew angry.

There in the bathroom, we invented all sorts of people who adore the sun.

The Cats

1

LET NO ONE TAKE HER AWAY—she's only a little cat. Dark fur: an aggregate of rich needles, each rounded, soft, and urchin-thick. Brook loved the cat, carried it out on the balcony. Her boyfriend is a cat! The kids yelled it on the block. She had moved to the city from another city and didn't know the people. She closed her curtains. She had named the cat Sis because there were similarities, facially, between her younger sister and the cat, as she told her mother once on the phone, before the mother sputtered "You're nuts!" then hung up, crying.

The cat had been a year old and wild when Brook found it, and never became fully domesticated. Whenever Brook grabbed Sis to brush the oily, dandruffy fur, the animal released adrenaline-soaked fear, even panting so its cheeks puffed, staring ahead, terrified, ears flattened, crying as if about to be murdered. But Brook brushed Sis assiduously. This made her recall the struggles, years ago, in brushing her sister's hair. Brook couldn't help adoring Sis, and loved to watch at mealtime when the animal was at its feral weirdest, dark lips and whiskers twitching, body startling, grunting above the food while purring, trying to eat before being eaten. When young, Sis had lived on an abandoned city block crawling with wildlife, even raccoons. So she must have learned to enjoy the condition—it really was an entire existence—of being not-devoured.

"She's only a cat, but I love her so much," Brook said to a man friend on the telephone. In a few days the man was gone, never calling again, which was fine, because Brook had Sis, and she told the cat everything.

As the most fragile object in Brook's home, Sis was not allowed to go outside, of course. The cat's wax-yellow eyes expressed wishes, expectations, and dislikes, Brook thought. But most often Sis lived in a continuous push-pull between her wildness and semi-domesticity: moving toward Brook, then bolting away, scared; later edging back to Brook's hand, then running, overtaken by the overwhelming fear of being close to a human being. Brook loved the wild cat's difficulty in trusting. She loved to be with the cat, as lovers famously want only to be with the other. Saying *I have to go home to my cat*, she felt proud in front of the shopkeepers on the street. *I have this responsibility*, Brook thought, and liked it. She could not tolerate the thought of Sis dying; the idea weakened her. Sis was already four years old. So she decided to have the cat replicated now, before it died.

Life is shockingly short, Brook told herself, sitting on the sofa in the afternoon, holding a tiny, white phone. Even a man or woman who is a celebrity among other human beings is not well-remembered decades after their passing, and so disappears. Brook held a pamphlet, around which ran a silver border, thick and continuous. Studying it, she breathed in reassurance. The Frinth Foundation of Life seemed benevolent. Named for its chief scientist who had died of the flu, the Frinth Foundation was not even wholly a foundation, Brook learned, now speaking to a receptionist or administrator; it was actually a company. No one person owned it, however, but this was very good, the woman explained, sneezing, because companies are stronger than foundations in certain ways, with broader or deeper watering systems for financial nourishment; and companies possess better armor overall, she went on, along with better ways to hide from the law, and so are less likely to die.

Squeezing the toothbrush-sized phone, dampening it, Brook asked questions. The administrator or representative, Mary, explained how the Frinth Foundation worked fruitfully along the border of life and death, and that while it encouraged life to ignite, nothing could really make life, the woman said, except the magic seeds themselves.

"Magic seeds?" said Brook, snorting.

"Well, that is one analogy we use," said Mary. "The Frinth Foundation of Life is not crassly commercial. It is difficult to find the language to describe what we do," she said. "It might even be easier using words from another language."

"But," Mary went on, "we want to get to know *you*, to fully screen *you*," and Brook felt warm.

After intake and instructions, it was nearly done. Brook closed the phone and stared through her large front balcony window at the change in season, which had brought a rotation of the senses. She was cold, and went to bed for the rest of the day and night, using not pills or encouragingly scented sleep-creams in order to relax, but instead, images in her mind of the new cat, the one to be born, an identical sister to Sis, who in turn was similar to Brook's real, troubled sister. It was a thought she liked: she, Sis, and the new cat, the three of them, playing, being weak together. The image pushed Brook close to some kind of far wall that retained almost the biggest feeling of her life.

She woke to the discomfort of the morning dark that pinched, because it was difficult, in the dark, to believe light would arrive, or that there was such a thing as light, as though she or the world had imagined it. The darkness seemed to make such an overwhelming statement against light; considering this, Brook dropped back to sleep.

In the Frinth Foundation of Life's consulting room, Brook was greeted not by Mary, but instead by a pale woman with freckles and a suit who handed her some paperwork and led Brook to an empty cubicle that may also have served as a short hallway. The place smelled of a cellar. Brook had brought the biopsy punch kit and, though the Frinth Foundation did not require it, a collection of Sis's hair and dandruff in a bank envelope, all of which she had scraped from the cat brush. Brook handed everything to the woman with freckles and a suit, who turned around and yelled "Charlie!" in a loud voice, and a long-haired girl about twenty appeared and took the envelopes, smiling widely at Brook, then at the wall, as she loped away.

The woman with freckles and a suit spoke, her voice soft and compressed, as if stored far back in her throat, beneath her ears.

"It'll be the initial twenty thousand," the woman said.

"I know that already," said Brook.

"Plus half the balance in October."

"Fine."

"And October is coming up soon," the woman said.

"I know when October is," Brook said, irritated.

"So," the woman said.

"I'll pay you if you give me somewhere to sit down!"

The woman went to a desk. "What," Brook said while paying, "if something goes wrong?"

The woman said the new pet was guaranteed. The animal would be delivered to her home in a fur-lined pet carrier at a time not yet specified, but long before winter arrived.

Brook wanted to talk more, but she did not know about what. As the company presented it, there seemed so few details, little to discuss. Where the white wall and the floor met, she saw a kind of extraneous, wavy flap, as if the wall were made not of plaster or board, but windblown fabric. "What if the new cat," Brook finally said, "doesn't remind me of my cat, Sis?"

"It will be a twin or like a twin," said the woman, "as you will see." She handed over some papers and a receipt, and Brook left the building, swarmed by cars.

2

WINTER DID NOT arrive easily, because the weather kept reverting to warm. Then the season pulled forward.

It was noon. Brook got out of the shower, her feet at their softest, pink and damp. Itching patches on her legs and arms, rooted far below the skin, blazed red, though showering helped relieve this. But she did not think about it; she was excited and impatient for the new kitten to arrive and wanted to tell someone. In her robe, Brook went to her back balcony, looking to the one next door.

"Hello," said Brook's neighbor, who sat there, a thin air of nastiness about her. Brook began to talk, describing how a new cat would be delivered to her home, though she refrained from mentioning that it would be a copy—a type of sister or daughter—of her own cat. She wondered what the neighbor woman, in her black robe, sunglasses, and flowered tiara, would say if Brook told the truth; perhaps she would just smile, as she was smiling now, her mind elsewhere. "So many cats have lived and died," the woman responded, rising from her chair. She said the Olympic games were now on television, and that she must go to watch them, and went inside. There are too many people in the world, Brook said to herself.

She stood near the new kitten, who waddled on the carpet. The big head bobbled uncertainly. It was soft and adorable, with its baby features. It pounced, moving constantly. Hiding under an end-table, Sis regarded the kitten miserably and hissed.

"Stop it, Sis," Brook said. "She's just like you, so be nice."

Yet the kitten was not identical to Sis. Its coat was lighter than Sis's, and it was not a shy pet in the least. These facts nagged at Brook; for the kitten seemed not the duplicate, but the opposite, of Sis. The kitten was a plump, happy creature, plus, Brook noted, its tail was strange. It was fluffy, not like Sis's slim tail, but ridiculously outsized, fuller and longer than a kitten's tail should be. The thing looked like a paddle, and collected fuzz from the carpet, making the tail look even bigger.

"I'll call the Frinth Foundation and give them hell," Brook said, irritated at everything, her skin itching besides. But she put off calling and spent the week in a routine of gym workouts and shopping for a luxury cat tree. She also focused on her hobby—written and sketched accounts of her night-time dreams, which were fantastic, like adventure stories that could happen to an astronaut.

It then occurred to Brook that if the kitten and Sis both died or ran away, or got burned up in a fire, she would have nothing left. So she began to collect clumps of their fur and their skin-flakes, storing these in two separate drawers of her bedside table.

3

BROOK WOKE FROM a nap, disoriented. It was noon. She lay there, thinking. The kitten was a disappointment. Brook did not like the way it sat on the couch with its mouth open, except it was not panting, its unwieldy tail lying there like a little fox beside it. And the creature had gained so much weight that its fur began to pull back, scant and sparse, on its belly.

She tried once to cuddle the creature, recalling that infants who are not touched by caretakers often wither and die. But the kitten had scratched her, and she dropped it on the floor. Lately, too, Brook had been ignoring Sis, though it was Sis's own fault, Brook reasoned: the older cat was too wild. Her constant hiding under the furniture was getting tiresome.

When Brook finally stretched and walked into the living room, she saw a small, decorative glass apple broken on the carpet into sharp chunks. The kitten's leg and flank were full of little bleeding wounds; thin blood trailed from its nose as it slept on the floor. Sis sat nearby, in plain view on the mantel, surprisingly, giving herself a noisy bath. Sis had a long gash on her flank, too, and it leaked.

Brook thought she might throw up. "What happened?" she cried, running around the room uselessly. "Did you both cut yourselves on glass? No, that couldn't be. Did you fight?" To the animals' silence, she said, "I never know what they think or do at all."

She cleaned both cats' wounds with a cucumber-scented cloth, and Sis struggled, running to hide under the couch. "Sis, if you attacked your sister, it's only because you're jealous," Brook chanted softly, waiting a moment, savoring the idea that Sis might compete with the kitten for her attention. She finished wiping away the kitten's blood, then felt something hard on its belly—a lump. "You have so many problems," she told the kitten.

In the following days, Sis's gash began to heal, but the kitten's wounds did not. Its gashes grew wider and more raw, bright red, even as the kitten played with bread clips and leaped almost as high as Brook's waist, making Brook laugh. The fur around the wounds had drawn back widely, too, so that areas of pink and dark skin now lay exposed on the kitten's flank and rear leg, though it was difficult to tell if these hairless areas were due to the kitten's continuing weight gain, or to the skin's way of dealing with the wounds. Either way, the patches of dry, bare skin had begun to spread toward the belly; they were now part of the animal's body's geography. Brook washed the hairless patches repeatedly with water and a new brown soap to encourage the fur to return, but in the end, only a few long, coarse, iron-colored hairs grew across the naked skin. At the same time, the animal's tail seemed to grow larger, bushier.

"I wish your tail would change. I wish your fur were different," Brook recited to the kitten, bathing it as it hung over her hand.

After the wounds disappeared, she began to touch the creature more, sometimes deliberately, in order to incite Sis's jealousy, for Brook had grown more attached to the strange-looking kitten, and had begun to care less for Sis. "Your sister is wild and confused. We can't really help her," Brook told the kitten, touching its bare, hot, large belly. "She's not much fun. But you're a darling. We'll take you to the vet soon, get some medicine for your skin." She picked up the heavy kitten, surprised how the animal seemed to reach out to wrap its arms and paws around her neck. The kitten hugged her and purred somewhat gaspingly. Its belly's skin lay burning against her. When anyone, a friend or someone closer, had disappointed Brook, she felt as if she barely existed anymore, had become transparent, maybe not having any organs of perception at all. Since the odd kitten already had let her down with its deficiencies, she knew it would not disappoint her further: a thrill went through her chest. "You're nothing but a dumb animal," she said into the creature's heavy neck.

Emerging from the shower, she shooed at Sis as the older cat shot past, skittish as ever. Brook sat on her blue chair and called the Frinth Foundation, rubbing the itching fingers that grasped the phone. "I want to know what's wrong with this cat, and I want it fixed now," she told the woman with freckles and a suit, describing the kitten's unhealed wounds and the raw, bare skin on its body that had spread, now seeming to dominate the kitten.

"Before delivering your pet, we did numerous tests that showed the kitten is physically fine and ready to live," said the woman.

"But she's *bald*," said Brook.

"Sometimes these animals have immune system suppression. This is temporary and can lead to lethargy or eccentricities. But the kitten is fine. One thing you might do is give her our vitamin powder—you blend it into a shake with avocado, which is extremely healthy and even necessary for cats. Cats that don't consume these ingredients are actually nutrient-deprived."

"You're telling me to give my cat milkshakes?"

"It is quite an adjustment to get this type of pet, Brook, especially if it's replacing a pet who died," the woman said. "You could consider writing in a personal journal or another outlet to explore your feelings."

Brook hung up. Ten minutes later, she called the Foundation again.

"I'm bringing the kitten to your office," she said angrily, "and I'll want to see your veterinarian right away, with no delays."

4

THE VETERINARIAN's office had a separate entrance around the corner from the Frinth Foundation, but the two businesses were intrinsic. Brook walked into the waiting room with her two cat carriers, at the last minute having decided that Sis should come see the doctor too. In bringing both pets, she could prove to the vet how drastically different the animals were, and how the replication process had cheated her. Even so, Brook thought, setting the carriers down, I would never give up this kitten, or reverse its birth. I love this kitten. The pets mewled loudly in their confinement, but grew quieter as Brook sat down. A man came through the door in a white coat and went to the front counter, looking at papers on a clipboard. In her anxiety, Brook stood and dashed to him, arms extended, stumbling accidentally into the man's chest, saying, "I don't know what I'm going to do if this kitten isn't cured!"

"Oh! You're not having a pleasant time of it, are you?" The man patted Brook's shoulder and, leaning against him, struggling to right herself, she patted him back; they stood in awkwardly close proximity as Brook stumbled again, falling further into the man such that her mouth pressed onto his coat, and she could not speak; the man's sympathy was clear enough, though, that Brook's eyes teared and she fell closer to him; the man said, his voice box vibrating at the top of Brook's head, "You know—I lost a big white shepherd just a month ago. And it is painful when a very large dog dies before you, the body being so large and all, plus, in death, it expands a little bigger, so that you're looking at an animal much bigger on the whole than it ever was, and in the case of a shepherd, even larger than almost any dog, but a little smaller than a small person…it's weird." The man drew back, and Brook saw his round, red cheeks. The man said, "Do you want me to look at your kitten?"

"I can pay you a special fee," Brook said, nodding, rubbing her face.

"No need," said the man, peering into the cat carriers.

"It started out as scratches from a fight they had," she said, "or maybe the cuts were from the glass apple." The man glanced at her. "This other cat, the adult one," Brook indicated, "She's not even a real pet. She's wild." Both cats meowed intermittently. "But when the kitten started looking so unwell, I got really upset!" she said, as if just realizing that was true.

"Of course," nodded the man. "That's a famous feeling!" His eyebrows rose infinitesimally as he stared at the kitten, saying only, "All right, then."

"How should we help her?" asked Brook.

"Well," he said, as if casting around. "You know, lots of strange things can happen. Now, we're all self-regulating animals, you see. The body's systems regulate marvelously, and really miraculously. It's kind of humbling. So at the same time, it's amazing that things ever go right! And we mammals being made of nearly 100 percent water," the man added cheerfully, "plus salt! Birds don't have saliva, you know. Isn't it funny to think that all our ideas and actions, and their consequences, come mostly from water and salt?"

Brook looked at the man, grinning on one side of her mouth, for his words had calmed her. His white coat was stained with coffee, as were his white tennis shoes.

"So you're the head veterinarian?" she asked, a bit flirtatiously.

"Oh, no," the man said easily; "I'm a baker. They're having a huge luncheon here at the foundation today, and we came to deliver the rolls through the back door."

"Jesus!" Brook yelled, stepping back. "Why did you make me think you were the doctor?"

"I didn't!" said the baker. "I—don't worry, it's okay." His cheeks flushed redder.

"It's not okay," Brook said icily.

"My name is Miles," the man said. "I'm sorry—"

"As if saying your name makes it all right?"

"—if I may have led you on for a moment."

"'May have'? Where's the vet?" Brook snarled.

"She might be in the party room, setting up the rolls," the baker offered.

"Oh, Christ!" Brook picked up both cat carriers, and Sis yowled.

Brook could trust no one, and could not stay here, not with the erupting sensation that she had no ground to stand on. She opened the door; she would phone the vet later.

"You should stay and see the vet, miss," said the baker. "The vet could help your cat."

The baker, who even had a light coating of flour in his hair strands, she now saw, who was holding the door open, who had just described for her the fragility and strength of life, made it hard—for there were still tree branches outside springing with green and flexibility in the winter wind—it was hard to leave, hard to stay. Brook thought of her strange patience in living with her cats, and the patience she exerted daily in knowing she was alone.

Sis cried again. In the enormity of creation, how was it possible that there was only one Sis, terrified and feral, unique in the universe? One was not enough.

But it must be enough. Brook glanced at poor Sis, who, with her waxen eyes and shiny, intelligent fur, possessed the light bearing of those who are without guilt. Both cats in their absence of speech and guilt, their dazzling humility, equaled birds, spiders, wolves.

"Ah," Brook said, standing in the doorway, to the cats, and to her acute disappointments. "Ah," she snapped. "I hate you."

"I hate you," she thundered to both cats and the baker. "What will we do?"

The Bean

IMAGINE BEING A BEAN: a pale supplicant, rimy dot, a belly-wrinkled pip, lying enervated on the kitchen chair, trying too hard all the time. He had a great green stalk of a father; steam from the oven reminded him of other beans who had died. What was it like, this propensity to roll, to fall on one's side? His hair stuck down. The days of the year rolled onward, proliferating in staggering numbers; they must have been a joke, a cushion designed to hurt his bones; the days would not stop. But the bean kept himself moist and adequate, as most do.

In school, he said he would never have a thesis statement, and from that moment he never did. Now, at his home, he lay on the chair, a stubborn, mealy creature, overly concerned about his lunch. He hated to go out of doors, preferring to rest and sleep, while his mother, a local bee, flew past the window frequently, and he knew how long passages of time, unpunctuated by his achievements, hurt her the most.

The bean looked away, ascetically sipping at the crevices of light beneath the door, startled by the rendezvous, midair, of his hands; and he would decide things later, and he would baste in thought: the dizziness of his lineage, the oily saturations he'd endured—

All the other beans had gone downtown for the night. He stared from the hill, stymied even by the nomenclature of himself, for he had too many parts: cusp and obdurate shell, rise of his puckered back, wrinkles dense as a baffle, eyes downturned; he was so full of excuses and the unorthodox comforts of shame, which he liked to fashion into a sensual, nighttime game; and he did not care to go downtown, though the others would be home soon; though in fact, the bean had traveled widely, albeit during an un-rememberable time.

The bean's name alone, spoken aloud, brought him shame. Atop his filament knees, the TV tray was full; he had playing cards too, and he was quite ready, pulling the very evening into his small, abraded lungs; he was prepared, though he had never yet said the words "providence," "tendril," or "dear." But he wanted to grow, and tomorrow he would, though when someone, for example a meter maid, chatted hello, he would reflexively strain, laughing too hard, then growing brusque and cold, usually operating at the far edge of his experience, his mother flying just outside the door, and in general, he was not particularly nice, though as his father once remarked, "Nice is overrated." And now, at the unquashable age of thirty-two, full of a hidden zest for parties, the bean lifted his heavy head, wishing intently to leave the house, but somehow he could not.

The bowl on his tray was filled with a thick, white soup. He had a compass and a pencil case too; on television a doctor once said, "It's simple to be yourself!" though actually, this turned out to be untrue, he realized in February, extending his threadlike arms, which contained, coincidentally, the prejudices of his mother who, long ago in full skirts, had fertilized the bean in a process which might be called "the lazy way out" (imagine being a bean, connected to no one, naked to the navel, lying on the chair, the vast articulations of the city, its people, all at such a hideous remove—).

He recalled the youth group meeting just a week before, where he had met a pretty pea who flirted with her bottom, yet the bean could not, on that day or any other, bring himself to speak to her, let alone kiss her with his opening. Then he saw how his veins flowed back. The best is to steal courage from others right along with their ideas, as a professor once said, and life allows for this theft so beautifully, yet the bean could not do this either, because right now, his mouth was burned from boiled tea.

Fear of tornadoes, insects, drought, mutton, gentiles, the all-delicious vegetable incitements of life; and the bean would never have his own house, he wept to himself; from the window he watched the others down in the city as they rilled from the bleachers and poured through the streets, striding together in rhythms of song, mouths open, dark and salutorious, hilarity their chorus, and all of them were awfully glad, for they had finished the spring semester, unlike he, who slept angrily with no pillow, grueling night it was, the juice of his body recirculating at dizzying speeds.

The Girl

THE GIRL WAS nearly a baby. She may have come from the suburbs (probably). She could have been born in one of the smaller cities; perhaps she had been ferried in.

Her hair was short and gathered to points, like whitish-brown fur. The girl stood in the hallway near the man who currently owned her, who kept her on a parents' leash. Most of the leash lay slack on the hotel's hallway floor, for the girl did not strain to its limit. She looked across the bare hall to the open stairway landing. Maybe the girl was foreign.

Even a few minutes after I first saw her I knew I would steal the girl. It was a leaden knowledge, like suddenly understanding the ending of a tale, show, or dream. Of course this dream was less about the girl (surely she was older than her body) than about the way I always had looked for something to raise me up, following the part of the story in which I had fallen.

The girl was so small she couldn't have mattered to anyone except her owner, whether or not he was her father. Even if he was, he would someday lose interest and replace her, I told myself. So it was natural that the girl should come with me.

The girl was about being poor and I was about the luxury of being able to choose—naturally, since the person closest to money always tells the tale or determines it. Our imaginations have been candied by glamour plots in which a rich lady or man finds a special waif to save. I had always heard and read this story and believed it true and even beautiful, so in a way I had fallen long ago.

I could leave the old hotel whenever I chose but waited, since I had gone there as punishment to myself. I had two credit cards in my pocket and that was all. My suit from work lay crumpled on the floor. The last few years, most of the decade, really, had frayed at some point and this made it somehow impossible for me to keep tidy or purposeful. So fixed like a molar in the chair, flush against the dresser, I sat for some hours with my door propped open, watching the hallway. From the outside I was barely visible, owing to the room's carpet and dark.

Even in my poorest, most anemic, lethargic parts, I was ready to save the girl and just for the relief of it. Besides, doing so would put me far above her man in the category of purity.

The man was severely tall and most often stood in the hallway with his friends. Everyone here stood in the hallways (the hotel rooms being unrealistically miniscule, the guests starved for company). The man was always talking and laughing and in his thinness there was strength, physical and otherwise. His voice was both loud and muffled, as if berries had been crammed into his throat. His cough was monumental. He would go back to Nevada, he said; he missed his big sister. He had lost his last chance to go driving in the hills with her; he would meet his sister. Other relatives had cheated him out of his inheritance money because they never had the decency to go by the rules. His mustache moved as if an entire puppet.

I didn't want to acquire an understanding of the man's life, or sympathy for him. The girl stood nearby in the tallowy light of the hallway, jaw open, breathing, mouthing words to herself, a half-game of half-boredom. I did not know if she was or was not some relative of the man's. It was hard to guess her age because of her pencilly bones, her underweight, her underbuilt nose. On floors above and below, folks moved through the fading hotel, arguing, shambling into rooms and out, finding each other for business on landings, trolling up stairs and back, not sleeping. Tattoos of coughs and occasional yelps beat past my ears as I waited to understand how to release the girl.

Coughs are gibberish, I told myself, dozing in the chair. When I awoke a few minutes later, I saw the girl through the doorway, her head dropped low: she was eating at an apple, leaving weird, cubic dental imprints in its core. She set this knobbed object against the baseboard, then sat back. She has some level of volition, I assessed. I thought I saw her heart beating through her chest.

With her strangely narrow face, the girl had exaggeratedly deep eye sockets and an abnormally small jaw. Occasionally her hands flapped up and down. She squinted; she can't see well, I told myself. Signs of a genetic disorder, I told myself, scanning her light irises. It was not clear to me if the girl was self-sufficient or could even comprehend social order. Was she smart, but unable to learn? I tabulated a mental page of such questions.

She seemed too young, flimsy, or tiny to stand or walk at ease, yet she did both. With her empty, tan, pleated dress, she divided the integers baby and girl. Between these poles lay gradations of identities I had not previously considered. Possibly she was both delayed and astute. For all her signs and symptoms, I didn't know what I was staring at; I needed to know. So I waited in the metal-framed chair and continued to hold the girl in my perspective.

I would give the girl what she needed (water, apples) for free; I would cut her dependence on the man and not only because I hated him. The details of this plan began to work through me, a kind of comfort meal that, after a difficult start, I began to digest.

I woke several times to reassure myself I would steal the girl to end her suffering. No one knows why even forest animals engage in altruistic acts, when they do. Helping others is only a confusion of identity, a ploy on the self, a rewinding of one's own life. The pleasure it brings is unreliable, a ruse.

The girl was brittle and on Sunday morning cried upon seeing the hotel manager burst through a door and run down the hallway with a clipboard squeezed to her breast. After this, the place was quiet again. Awake for a few minutes, I wondered with a trickle of drama if the girl would be able to survive until I took her away.

But at sunset, when more fully awake, I pinched open my door to see the girl was just the same, dawdling nearsightedly along the walls. She and the man were standing out there, and even before I noticed the climate of sex between them I already had begun to feel left out. As he spoke to her quietly (without pausing—an inane monologue, I told myself), the girl did not object. The leash was not in sight. They must have grown closer, I told myself, and when I watched him sit down on the floor next to her, my jealousy really unfurled. I returned to the room and began to collect my clothes. The man may even have begun as the girl's school teacher, I told myself, eventually unable to contain himself in light of her deficits, of the erotics coursing at all times beneath teacher and student, a wide, pulling river. Then too the man must have had inside him a furious strain of defiance.

I got dressed at last. The girl was tracing circles with her forearms and elbows on the walls and the man was telling the hotel manager (timid-looking, still squeezing the clipboard) about some other man who was not at the hotel and who was considered a cheating liar. The girl wore beads in the shape of mice around her neck—blue, pink; with her elfin, hyperextended fingers she swatted at them. Another man in the hallway, grinning unkindly, bent down to hand the girl a metal cup, huge in her hands. She took it and sniffed, as if to drink, then dropped the cup (empty) on the floor, pacing on. Others in the hallway either ignored her fully or gave her a large margin, bringing to mind the word *invalid*.

In my wrinkled work suit and high, tight shoes, I left the room.

Some women don't like being one and that goes for me. There is the restlessness and endless vigilance that arises from working constantly alongside men. Though occasionally (in a rush) I fasten on to one of them with a movement somewhere between a trip and a fall, desire being the wish to transform into someone else, a different kind of body, to find another story in which to live.

I was surprised at the tininess of the girl's face close up: a pinprick. She was wholly unimpressed by me. Our mute introduction did not exactly ring with warmth. She glared. Toward this near-jawless, silent, birdy object, I felt nothing. I picked up the girl and ran. My shoes could have been quieter. I did not look back to see if the man with the berry throat had witnessed this action, but clasping the girl beneath my arm, I fled downstairs.

If the girl ever had possessed any significant body weight, she had lost its burden at this point. She was as if a layer of gauze, so light, I realized, I easily could have taken her days before without any concern over how to bring it off. It would have been similar to stealing a cruller. Perhaps she was truly ill. I ran, carrying her, through the hallway downstairs, then back up the staircase to the third floor, around a corner, and to my room.

The girl's lightness poured through me. I locked the door and paced the floor, drinking in a wide, edgeless pleasure far beyond any that usually arises from helping another person. I was pulsing with it and the air I breathed was scented of melon, satiety. I set the girl on the white bed sheet.

I waited, still brimming with the pleasure, and soon, because I wanted to know, I asked. "How old are you?"

"Way older than five," she hissed. The voice was rageful, like mine.

The conversation stalled there. I watched her sit there, eyelids slipping open and shut. The girl scarcely had a life; I told myself this probably made her an expert at some things. She might be a person who someday would sing beautifully. But the time for her to sing had not yet arrived.

Her eyes flickered. The sum of her faulty, inherited, heritable symptoms, her entire smallness, made her perfect for me (I told myself). I believed she matched my bumps and shallows. The need for the girl was strong.

I wafted the door open. The man with the berry throat was now in the midst of telling a story as the others stood around variously. He could cook eggs in a way that beat out everybody else's, he said; the eggs came out like clouds. He could melt butter, he said, with creamed almonds into cake so that everyone wound up loving him at all gatherings on all Sundays. In some remote way he was mocking himself and this talk was a play for the others to appreciate his self-deprecation. I began to get a headache. The man was laughing, scrubbing a blue shirt back and forth around his waist. He loved to nourish other people, he said. He had not yet noticed the girl's absence. The hotel manager with her clipboard, resting against a doorjamb, sent the man a clayish, desirous smile, which he did not see.

I closed the door. The girl was with me (unbelievably) and I did not know what would happen next. The end of the story usually is determined by something near the beginning. The girl looked away from me and I knew she would stay quiet. I went close and examined her dress, her neck. I pulled back the neckline of the dress. To the side of the girl's sternum lay two pink crisscrossing weals, which formed a raw X. I let go of the dress and she lay back with stiff arms, eyes closed. Her chest vibrated, a slight buzzing like an alarm. A few seconds later the chest buzzed again. A pacemaker, I realized, and a badly installed one at that. Its clock-like shape visible beneath the skin of her chest.

The girl was nothing like me, I was certain. The hem of her slubby dress covered her shins. Her light canary eyes settled on me and instantly, without words, told me about the man with the berry throat, the person with whom she probably had spent the most time. In a broad language of hues, her eyes told me the man had whims (of course) and that he gave her hurts, candy-sweet, lots, all sorts. As I understood the language, I became the man. It was neither easy nor hard. It must have happened because the girl, or part of her, wished it. The man's impulses and chaos chased over my skin, everything moving faster; I wanted to do things to the girl, turn her upside down, yank her around because that had been his way and now it was mine. I wanted to move her around in even tastier ways.

I stood up from the bed and looked at my forearms. From nature comes the gift of self-recognition and the core of the self, which really exists (a notion I once would have scorned). I knew myself and my life—not too arduous a study. I had grown up, left home, and gone to work. Being without a family, I became less real, which is the biggest cliché of the story but true.

I had no intention of really becoming the man, so I sloughed him off me (easy). I strode around the room and praised myself for ridding myself of his recklessness. My skin rang out beautifully because all along I had been the better one, the one who would never hurt a girl.

The man with the berry throat now understood I had the girl. He pounded at the door and began scraping his hand on the small window to the left of the door. His face appeared in the gap of window that the curtain left. He turned then and began a tremendous coughing fit. I was unable to stand up and pull the curtain shut; I just sat squeezing my hands. Then the man recovered and must have wedged his feet inside the door frame, because I heard him climbing upward. In a few moments his head appeared in the door's transom window. I hid my eyes, whining, knowing the man's face was up there, looking in, and the mass of my life's incessant errors filled me up. Whereas only minutes before, the girl's lightness had filled me.

When he saw her on the bed, the man began yelling "Dammit!

Godammit!" through the window. His voice was full of nerves. I finally ran to hit the light switch on the wall, eliminating his power to see the girl. I told myself that his life's errors had ruined him more badly than my errors had ruined me. He pressed the side of his head against the glass, yelling further, then dropped down to the floor. There he pried at the door's lock. I could hear his breath and fury. Suddenly the girl sat up at the edge of the bed and spat out, "What, Jason?"

"Ritter!" he screamed through the door. "Don't you even think about it, don't even!"

I picked her off the bed and ran to the back window, enjoying the chance to carry the girl's lightness again. Two feet below: a breezeway leading to the street. I forced her sharp cheek to touch mine. The clock-like thing inside the girl helped her heart pound along, clumsily marking the time I had saved her from her former life's burdens. If clocks and time-keeping are merely agreements between people, it is also true that all bodies are clocks (I told myself); and all clocks bear the paradox that they must both oscillate and be precise. Behind me, from the hotel's hallway, I heard the man yelling again. The girl's head wobbled slightly as I held her. I jumped down to the breezeway and ran. She was made of little more than mesh, oddly shaped; the wind circulated around us. We fell into the back seat of a cab as it shot away.

I told the cab north to Los Angeles. Things move quickly in the parts with suspense because our appetites have been stirred and the body (the mind) itches to finish. But I already knew the outcome of this dream. The ending is usually less the point than the middle.

We drove up a hill to some rocky land undisturbed by dwellings. The cab's music became loud, dark, crazily fast, scabbed all over with hundreds of beats per minute. Then the cab raced into a skein of roads locked with cars. Los Angeles is always out of hand, I remembered, and you put up with more than you thought possible. But a college-aged boy stood on a sidewalk, wearing only a T-shirt to his knees, fencing the air with a desk lamp; the girl laughed at this pantomime (birdily), to my surprise. I willed the boy to fence the air again so that the girl and I could laugh together.

The cab tore on. "Have you gone to school?" I asked, and felt like a buffoon.

The girl was quicker than I had realized. Her eyes rolled sarcastically in her recessed skull. "Not recently," her voice buzzed nastily.

The conversation ended. I could not think of another question. It is so easy to lose the mark. I wondered if the girl might need some kind of daily medication regimen. I still had the credit cards. Then I realized I must feed the girl at some point, so I directed the cab west toward a drive-through market.

A few minutes later I tore open a grocery bag: mayonnaise, fish, seeds. The girl glanced at me, then devoured all of it, gulping like a centaur. I watched the meal travel through her stalky throat. Particles of food jumped from her face as she chewed noisily, surveying the interior of the cab, squinting outside at the sun. The girl was really enjoying herself. Being alive is its own reward.

After the meal she settled back and amid short, jagged, inspiratory breaths, she stared out the window quietly—perhaps now the girl was privileged (fed) enough to begin to feel sad. After awhile she took the grocery bag, looked in, and opened it to show me; my knees shook for the tidy, determined way she looked at me. There is no point in struggling to change the outcome. At the bottom of the grocery bag lay a string of figs. Ah, a dessert thrown in by the cashier, I thought, reaching in. But in my hand, the string flopped open unpleasantly and wriggled with so much heft that I flung the thing on the cab floor. It was the leash (I told myself). The girl lunged for it. "No!" I commanded, the third sentence I ever had spoken to her.

"I want that," she said.

I kicked the thing under the front seat and pushed her to prevent her from leaning down; she reached over with her rubbery mouth and bit me. I shrieked and blew steam; the cab bumped all over the road; she bit harder, beginning to drool.

"What the hell are you doing?" I yelled.

"What the hell are you doing?" the girl said with her tiny, recessive face as she released me. I couldn't help laughing for the closeness of her imitation. The tooth prints in my forearm filled up with blood.

"I want that," she repeated, eyes searching for the string.

It wasn't a leash, I knew. But I could not allow it. "No," I said.

The girl grunted something to the effect of me going to hell. Now on the freeway, the cab picked up tremendous speed. She leaned away, resigned, eyes closed. The tips of her hair blew back and I saw her heartbeat in the artery of her neck. I wondered how long the girl would live. But before she aged and eventually died, she might grow. She might even learn to speak more fully, and so I would need to reply.

Months later, when she was gone, I sat inside another taxi north of Los Angeles, challenging the driver for a long time over my fare, and as I paused a moment to restructure my argument, I saw a gray, matted cat crouching on the sidewalk. The cat was old and cast off, with a bad eye. I remembered how long I had been separated from everyone, and I remembered the girl, whom I never understood and whom I had tried to steal.

The Wedding

HALLO. I'M A FOOL. I married Mike Sump. We had a green-colored wedding. I was sick, the whole room turned green. They took me home. Was I married, I wanted to know, looking up at them. They pulled me on a stretcher. I was home, all alone. The walls rang in stillness. And the kitchen, motionless, all afternoon. Was I married? I didn't know. Everyone was gone. The sun bore down. Newspapers turned yellow. My stomach swelled.

I lay on the floor, staring up. Sunflowers hung outside the window, huge as leeches, unrestrained. The serenading music was gone. There was much disappointment. There was a secret pattern of right and wrong. And one could not know.

A nurse came through the door.

"Life is quite naturally a whirlwind!" she said cheerfully and began to give me a bath.

"Stop it," I breathed. The nurse ignored me. She wiped a cloth down my spine. The smooth water was hateful and so was the satisfaction that anyone ever had known.

"Am I married?" I asked.

"Oh, you've got to keep to the marrow of things, you've got to rein yourself in," sang the nurse. "Keep the bile in your stomach, girl, and never throw a grain of salt away. Are you married? Yes, since the day you were born."

She lay me down like a board. The time of day was unclear. My ankles were beautiful and I could not look. I looked to the nurse.

"That's not true. I was a little girl once. I wasn't married then."

The nurse only smiled and hummed. She wiped me dry.

"Is the wedding over?"

"Christmas, no! —They're dancing like pigs over there, and in deep trouble with the police as well!"

Lying below the window I watched the crows in the sky.

A question occurred to me. "Why am I at home? I'm not sick anymore."

"All lives begin in a home," the nurse said. "It's what everyone dreams of."

"Where will I sleep?"

"Here in the kitchen, right here."

I began to sob. "But what will I do with my life?"

"You'll be a journalist!" cried the nurse. "You'll say things that aren't true. Isn't that what you've always wanted? Please, you must do it. Otherwise..."

"Otherwise what?"

"...it will grow to be spring and summer without you, dear." The nurse folded a towel. She looked away.

I remained on the floor. There seemed no way to begin. Above me, the wind puffed the curtains gently. Outside, the movements of insects on their egg sacs were miniscule. There was a taste of metal to the air. There was an absence of liberty that one could not destroy.

I looked up at the nurse. She had sweet, glamorless eyes. I asked: "Where is Mike Sump? I have to talk to him."

"He loves you. Why should you talk to him? You're married now. He'll work at the ice rink."

"When can I get up?" I cried.

"It's so difficult to love, isn't it?" she answered, hands on her lap.

The nurse stood. "Lord, I'm exhausted," she said. She removed her smock. She lay down and seemed desperate to sleep. Like an infant she clenched the blanket. "There's such a terrible tension that exists between being alone and being owned," she whispered. I stared at the nurse. She closed her eyes. The silence was vast. Night came. Far away, I heard the sounds of the wedding. In the air hung a thirst for knowledge, already undermined.

The Wolf

A NEUROLOGIST, in the middle of summer, holds a warm beer in one hand and a desiccated grapefruit rind in the other. It is true. He sits in the dry mud, west of Chehalis.

He is past youth, wearing a tight beard and glasses. Problematically, he has begun to have spells in which he feels he does not exist. The doctor lives in the city, near the hospital where he works.

But facts quickly metamorphose into tales. Is it sometimes, or most of the time, that he wears the hideous oat-colored Birkenstocks? Does he know exactly why he has driven away from the city, alone?

Even in the voluptuous heat near the river, the doctor wears a tight, buttoned blue shirt. The sun makes his scalp livid, puffy. No wet towel on his head, no plans to fish in the rust-colored river? But he is distraught. He pours the half-beer on his head. His name is Fred.

A tale looks to the past for balance, resonance. Fred has long had a home, and a marriage, such as it is. Children. A garden full of herbs, coffee grounds, manure.

Long ago, Fred experienced a professional zenith when, as a surgical resident, he realized it was not such a big deal to make an incision into a patient's body. Pull the blade down through the layers of skin—very simple. Then the healing work can begin. Fred was thrilled; he used the realization to impress girls. The scalpel is a form of freedom, he told himself.

Now, years later in the woods near the river, Fred has poured beer on his head. An act of self-dislike? Fred has gotten pissy with his wife, has begun reading books about self-reinvention. The wife has moved out, buying a downtown condo with a balcony the size of a tweezers.

Carefully placing her feet on this balcony, Fred imagines, the wife will look at other vacant balconies. She will look down to mauve pigeons, pavement, summer rain.

For Fred, it's the episodes of feeling he doesn't really exist—how to shake these? Why does he feel he is disappearing? He stands, walks back toward the woods, tossing the grapefruit skin. Blazes of mosquitoes. The rich thud of his shoe on the path. The tale's progress is more certain now. He moves through the trees, spots an abandoned shed. Looking through a broken window, Fred sees, standing upright, a wolf.

The wolf sidles out of the shed, smiling invitingly, even seductively, in the way that other species can render us smitten or transfixed. The wolf stinks of pelt, fungus, putridity. But Fred is excited. He must phone his wife. The wolf sashays into the woods; Fred follows—how could he not?—and jabbers into his cell about a wolf. He feels wonderful now, more like his old self. *What is the wolf?* he whispers into the phone. In maladjusted, yet joyful strides, he tears through the trees, knowing if he touches the wolf, he might be overcome, lose control in a seizure of happiness and gorgeous self-regard. The tale is about opportunity. We live amongst rich possibilities.

The Danas

Two people owned a house. The house was gray, soft to the eye as ashes. It was large, even containing a low, windowless bedroom near the cellar. The man and woman who lived in the house had never even found this little room. Yet that in itself was not an inappropriate failure.

The couple was named Mike and Tina Dana. None of the Danas' string-haired children ever had tried a thing in life, including hiking, second languages, or flying; nor had the children ever tried dying from any cause. Mike and Tina Dana's own parents had not tried it, either, so the entire clan lived—a genetic current, a proteinous statement of form, the envy of neighbors—under Mike and Tina's pinnacled roof that vaulted through time.

During the holidays, when weather was darkest, Mike and Tina Dana gave their family home-cooked, sweetened milk in jars, relieved that none of them would accept any foreign, outlandish gifts, but only this simple gift of milk; and from reading certain magazines and pamphlets, the Danas learned, and were apt to argue, that milk sugars were the only appropriate nourishment for human brains.

Mike and Tina Dana usually wore large, white, thick bathrobes. They had practically finished rearing their oldest set of children. All of it—the living—had happened so quickly, thought Mike Dana from his chair, picking at the skin of his knee, gazing at his eldest son and daughter, who were two years apart, sitting together on the sofa with their finely-knit, coppery complexions and tawny hair. The two conferred quietly, sharing a soft cotton bag their mother had packed with snacks. These older children had always been quiet, even before birth, when they had existed only as streaks of bruise and absence in their mother's psyche.

But now, the two eldest had gotten so awfully tall and mature that it was nearly frightening, as Tina Dana recently had confided to the mailman through the door slot.

The harvest season had arrived, with its cool scents and rotations of storms. So Mike and Tina Dana made it known that it was time for grandchildren. As the oldest son and daughter murmured together on the couch, the Dana parents, along with an assortment of aunts and other relatives, gathered in the kitchen and its long hallway on this important day. The family pinched their fingers, the soft skins of their forearms; no one dared speak. Finally, the news rippled down the hall, and Mike and Tina Dana jumped up with delight in their bathrobes and shouted. Their eldest son and daughter had announced that they would finish school in December, then quickly marry each other; they would begin their own family. Tina Dana leaped off the step-up to the dining-room, arms bound tightly around herself as if to squeeze tears from her eyes. For a long moment, her exultant cry filled the house. Happiness was a wash of color; it was theirs.

All relatives, including the youngest children of the family, spoke giddily that afternoon, toasting, making plans, celebrating. It was exciting in a grand way until, oddly, the young look-alike couple, from deep in the sofa, informed the nearest gathered relatives that, once married, they would move out of their parents' home and rent an apartment three blocks away.

The moment they heard this news, Mike and Tina Dana grew purple and near-sick with rage, for they wanted their children to be at home always. White bathrobes wilting, heads bent, they grew aggressive, shoving all relatives, including an aunt and a cousin in wheelchairs, out the back door. Stricken, the Danas spent the night yelling and crying because their oldest children's move threatened the family with a kind of destruction and calamity that previously never had been known. In the nerve-ridden tumult of the next few hours, the entire clan also feared some second, unknown, undertowing disaster, since one catastrophe usually clears the way for the next.

Sunk into the sofa, the two eldest managed to hold firm: they would move out and rent an apartment. As day became night, their mother went to bed and quickly contracted double pneumonia because of the news. The ashen young couple, unable to get up, spent the night on the couch below the coughing mother's room, their arms and legs entwined, hair soaked, bleating intermittently in half-sleep. When the boy began to show the symptoms of a cold, the girl, as was usual, caught it from him within a few seconds, since the pair was so close and confused with their bodies.

The children remained unwell, not able to stir at all, but Tina Dana recovered from her illness quickly, bounding from bed at 5 a.m. the next morning, bare-footed, searching the refrigerator for chicken.

Somehow, though, the Dana family survived. Life began to acquire a shaky rhythm. Time, a disinterested party, yanked forward, with daylight and its alternating twin, darkness, forming what seemed a large-scale joke, a puzzle, through which the Danas—the entire neighborhood—had to maneuver.

While the young couple crept from their apartment back to their house of origin every day for breakfast, lunch, and dinner, the three-block distance remained a painful insult to the parents, who needed so much more.

Soon, though, all relatives began to focus on the new baby to be born someday, knowing that the child's skin, his mindbreakingly lovely scent, would be recruited to soothe the family's conflicts and disturbances for years to come. And certainly, everyone knew, the child would grow up to be a genius; he would have to, for the family was relying on it; or else he could be a girl.

Through a living room window covered by a thick, beige curtain, the Danas' next-door neighbor, Mrs. Beck, peered at the Dana house with interest and fury. She had seen the young brother-sister couple arriving on the doorstep, greeted by their parents with bowls of soft eggs. Mrs. Beck sweated along her neck. She felt the Dana family was bad.

"Why?" She asked her companion Janice-Katie. "Why should the son and daughter start their own family? Instead, they could travel the country separately and develop new interests."

Janice-Katie leaned against a doorjamb. Spring was the time of year she felt most alone. She said, slowly, thinking, "Well, I suppose the Danas just love each other so much that they cannot bear new people, or new situations, besides their own. They keep to themselves, have you noticed?"

"Cripes, yes! It burns me up," said Mrs. Beck.

"Everyone in that family is so loving that each knows the exact whereabouts of the others at all times," Janice-Katie reported. Have you heard them in the yard, calling to each other at night?"

"Have I," said Mrs. Beck.

"You see, to them, outsiders are not good," Janice-Katie explained. "The Danas want the family to keep together, because that is the most important thing to them. They don't like the splits in seams, or separations."

"But anyone can see that family is just too close," said Mrs. Beck, fingers squeezing the window frame. Her body emanated a great heat of combustive wishes and frustrations.

"They are just an exceptionally devoted family—what of it?" Janice-

Katie said, sinking to the sofa, reaching for a colorful magazine about young people's lives and clothes. She put the magazine back down. "I suppose most of us were simply never loved, and will never be loved, with the intensity that the Dana children are loved. That is just one of life's compromises, I'm afraid."

Only yesterday, her purse accidentally had upended. Some yellow potato chips and pencils even had spilled mutinously along the sidewalk so that Janice-Katie had to retrieve them, along with a lone rolling mint, at the center of downtown. And some sleeping pills and ladies' products she knew she must throw away when she got home, for everyone there on the street—her neighbors—watched these drop to the ground. The moment growing more crucial without her consent, Janice-Katie had looked up at the passersby with her trademark sarcasm. "Oh, this is just beautiful, just what I love, everything I own spilling on the ground!" she said loudly for the others to hear. A rumpled-looking man, poor in some way—she had never seen him before—stood nearby on the sidewalk with a brown suitcase.

When nearly still a child, Janice-Katie had learned that an edge in her jokes could make others laugh. It lifted a burden away from her, so she had cultivated it at home, the place where, without warning, cruelty could cut her the most. Sometimes she felt the sarcasm clinging around her eyes and mouth like a plastic film gathered on her face. She did not realize that this layer did not truly conform to her contours until the man with the suitcase stood looking at her critically, as if she were a clown or insane.

That was yesterday, and even today she bore a light mantle of shame.

"The whole family!" Mrs. Beck said. "I woke last night and couldn't go back to sleep, thinking of all of them. Have you seen the older children lately? They look so dry—like leaves. They should drink more water and be more active. You don't think they know who I am, do you?" The foggy shape on the window near Mrs. Beck's mouth contracted, as if trying to grow alive, separate from her.

Janice-Katie said, "Irene, you're ruminating."

It seemed to her that, lately, she and Mrs. Beck did not merely live next door to the Danas, but—neither woman could help it—in response to them, too.

"Bad people make me mad," Mrs. Beck said. "I've been that way since I was little."

Janice-Katie drifted toward the stove with a wish she could not identify and so decided it was thirst. "I could put something cold into a cup," she said aloud.

Mrs. Beck did not hear. At the window, still uncomfortable, staring at the Dana's multi-storied home, she cleared her throat, where the jealousy most prickled.

In another house on the street, a woman was finishing a popular puzzle in her bedroom, hunched over with a pencil in concentration and pleasure. She looked up for a moment. Sally Christie had heard everything about the Danas through neighborhood talk, and, though generally cautious to avoid the family, she also was avidly drawn to them.

Sally said to herself, "I guess those two oldest Dana children are not really to blame for being such wilted specimens. But instead of getting married so young, why, they could get college degrees, then come back home and work in community leadership! Our town needs young people to stay here and contribute."

Earlier, she had discussed the matter with her husband, who said, "If you tell me that the Dana children are poor, innocent things one more time, I'll just spank you, Sally Christie. Innocence is an illusion—made up by society."

"You are such an intellectual, Jose," said Sally, accustomed to the man's declarations.

"Almost no one really is innocent," the husband said. "It's a sentimental idea. Even tiny children can learn codes of ethics."

Sally smiled, making her eyes flat discs, unwilling to think about the matter.

"The point is," the man said, "the Danas *are* off-track. Anyone who makes their children stay at home for so long—well, Mike and Tina Dana are just trying to avoid being alone together, it's plain to see. And that's just weak," he finished firmly, touching the leaf of an aloe plant.

Sally stretched out her legs, pointing her feet along the sofa. "But, can you imagine if *we* had two sets of children, one older, one so much younger, just like the Danas have? It would be like having two separate families!" she said, flushing.

"Hmm, we could open a hotel," said the husband.

"At an older age, to have more children...I would love it...wouldn't you? Wouldn't you?"

If she spoke with anxiety and hope, it was because she was free to do so with her partner in their fragile home. Along with this, she could count on him to put her to bed when fathoms of tantrums overtook her and made her scream in the bathroom. The sounds of loss and desperation were never far from her mind.

"Babies? Nonsense," the husband said, biting into a piece of food.

"I am going to my bedroom," said Sally.

But that was earlier. Now, holding the puzzle book, she startled, for her son, aged four, walked into the room. The boy's hair was messy and, seeing him, Sally felt a crush of adoration and pain, as if she had lost him already.

The boy was usually aloof, which frightened his mother. "Come here," she said, reaching for him. The boy ran to a corner. He still wore diapers, and his plastic pants swished. "I like games," he told her, "and other kids. I don't like sauce, and grandpa. That's how I am."

Sally was stunned now, as every day, by the child's autonomy. "But, don't you like me, dear?" she asked, her heart in her voice.

"No," said the boy.

"Don't say that—because—do you hear me?" Sally was surprised that she took a hairbrush and smacked it loudly on her hip.

The child slithered away. "Mommy?"

She went to him, pressing his face on her pants leg. "I'm sorry, dear. Please, just...don't ever forget Mommy," she said, squeezing the boy's shoulders, her emotions blotting out, for a moment, her usual reserve and entire mind. "Someday, when you're grown up and go away, I will miss you so much."

The boy disengaged from her and, with the graceful movement that was native to him, went to retrieve a plastic sheep that was behind a chair. "Oh, do not worry," he said.

"I am more helpless than I ever dreamed, since him," she thought, staring at herself and the child in the wall mirror.

After putting him to bed, she adjusted her blouse, her defenses solid again, and looked through the curtain at the Dana's house, with its large, windowless side wall of gray brick.

"I would never speak to any of them," she thought. "The last time was on Halloween. The Danas are not for me.

"But—what if all the neighbors got together and knocked on their door? If we told Mike and Tina Dana that their two oldest children had gone away to the city, had suddenly run away, just as a trick?"

The idea brought Sally a great deal of satisfaction, but she did not pursue the thought. She drew back from the window and found other things to do that day. After all, she had spent much of her life fending off wild ideas, and was fairly expert at it. "The Danas are my neighbors, nothing more," she said to herself that night in the smoothness of her bed sheets.

Alia

IN OLD FAIRY TALES, a white bird signifies renewal and hope. A hero may go through gradations of trials in order to find the reward of a white bird, which denotes a treasure. And the treasure is oneself.

Madja's uncle owned one of those birds—a cockatiel. Madja was my roommate at school. She always exhibited a cool, martial quality. Many young girls are soothed by meticulousness, authority, and rules. In Madja's case, this identification did not fade as she grew older. Her clothing was simple and ironed, and her mahogany hair sloped into the shape of an elongated bowl. The clean angle of her chin mesmerized me.

Each year we were at school, Madja was assistant floor resident, her position apparently unassailable. One night, Madja told me about her Uncle Lee as we sat in the metal-framed dorm chairs. As I listened, I wanted to have been her, to have had, growing up, an uncle who owned a white bird, to have gone to the uncle's house, to have eaten lunch there, to have slept on the couch as the TV blurred. Night would have filled up the bare windows at the rear of the house, and I would have looked down to the skyline on the river, where Midwestern office buildings grew starry inside with light. The uncle's bird would hunker nearby, with its uncanny ability to speak our language. The mechanism of speech being maze-like and incomprehensible, inviolable as a jewel.

I remain convinced of nothing. But on the night Madja described her Uncle Lee, I became his niece. Flat and coin-like, I tumbled toward the family—the uncle, his bird, and also the brothers and youthful parents Madja had described. As I fell into the circuitry of their relationships, a current closed over me and I was theirs. I knew everything about the family. Before anything else could transpire, I clipped Madja out of the scenario and tossed her aside because I was the niece, not she.

I set up camp in Uncle Lee's spacious TV room, with its whorled rock pattern on the linoleum floor. My uncle lay back in his recliner, watching Cardinals football, and next to him, the parrot inched atop its cage. Uncle Lee had magnificently thick, white hair. His rough, red hands' texture recalled the bird's chicken-like feet.

Uncle Lee had named the bird Alia. She had spoiled eyes. Loaded with pretty seeds, the bowls on Alia's perch were fresh and tidy. She stretched one wing, then the other, showing off, for after all, Alia was loved, and she was proud. Her little body was puffy with a sense of security and belonging. The sound of Lee's name was inside the bird's. He carried Alia around all the time. She stirred my longing because she was not human, but even so, her self-confidence annoyed me.

The room was cool and darkish. I had grown younger. This was a calmer, slower era than the one from which I had come; there was no fear or mean-spiritedness emanating from the TV. Lying on the black vinyl couch, I was as warmly cocooned as a family member could be.

Steam from a simmering dinner eked down the hallway. Then a metallic banging, a cuss.

Uncle Lee and Aunt Laura fought all the time. That was the downside of visiting their home. I did not speak much to Aunt Laura. She was sour. Lee worked on and off for an airport car service; the lack of a more promising job enraged Aunt Laura and it seemed she could not dispel that feeling. It tore at her, and her face seemed to grow smaller over time.

In any case, it was the bird who was Uncle Lee's bride. He pulled a wooden paddle from behind his chair so Alia could climb on it. He brought her new toys; he petted her; I watched them together. The man kissed her streaked gray beak; the bird smothered his forearm with her pebbly tongue. She whistled, the intensity of her birdy adoration focused on the older man. "Oh hey come on!" she said.

"Alia da queena!" Uncle Lee roared. Curled on the couch, I smiled.

"I didn't know you could make yourself so small, kid," Lee hollered at me, stalking from the room, Alia on his shoulder. Down the hall, he yelled that Aunt Laura had not visited his mother. Laura yelled back that it was a filthy chore to visit Lee's mother, and if he wanted her to visit the woman so badly, then she, Laura, would quit making dinner and go out for a good drink besides. The stove fan stopped humming. I heard Laura's shoes stamp the floor.

"Oh, you go right to hell, Laura!" Lee screamed alarmingly. He returned to the TV room, checking the game. Silhouetted in the TV light, Alia swung around my uncle's fingers, whistling in pleasure, not seeming to notice the yelling. "Try some, you will," the bird said. Alia often uttered fragments from TV advertising.

Aunt Laura appeared in the doorway, her stalky throat moving, swallowing. In her short skirt and blouse she held a teapot and set it on a TV tray in front of Lee. Her mouth was a pen line, and with an air of defiance, she poured the drink for us all.

We drank in the tea's strong, leathery taste. Its astringency pulled our energy from the evening hours that lay ahead and into the immediate present. My heart whirred; the moment dilated. I realized a gigantic marital battle was about to ensue. Only Alia remained in a more normative present, unaffected by the fuel-like tea, bobbing her head, squeezing Lee's arm with her feet. "Seven-two-one!" she said. Lee set the bird on the floor and she waddled across the linoleum, babbling.

Not even having begun, the fight already confused me. The horizon grew dusty. Perhaps the fight was overdue, and my aunt and uncle needed its spectacle for the distance and release it would bring. Maybe the nasty, divisive outcome of the fight would feel like destiny to Lee and Laura. I thought: this is preventable. Yet neither my aunt nor uncle cared to look into themselves or their marriage. People are not more than who they are, so in fact the fight was not preventable. The only truth was that Lee and Laura's marriage produced poison.

And I was here with them, lucky to even know about the poison. When you have no one, even the most potent toxin is fresh water.

Lee threw a white glass ashtray on the floor. He asked Laura, yelling, why she had flirted with some third party at a shrimp-tasting exhibition. Laura scoffed—it was nearly a scream—and made her own accusation.

I raised myself from the couch, looking for my car key, realizing I owned no car, not now. But Uncle Lee had a car. I scooped Alia up on the wooden paddle and headed for the spare bedroom down the hall. The bird whistled in alarm.

"Where the hell you going with my bird, kid?" Lee gruffed at me. But his eyes were on the enemy, Laura.

"Good girl!" said Alia.

The fight powered on. "You simple, asinine, useless cripple," Laura stated, as if reading from a shopping list. "You'll shut your goddamn mouth when I finally kill you!"

"Oh, ohhh!" Lee mocked. I could not stomach the fight. I found a key ring heaped in a candy dish and ran out with the bird, trying to shield her with my left arm. In the deep autumn cold, the leaky garage window's curtain was rigid with streaks of ice. I blasted the car heater. Alia squawked. She clung to the back of the car seat, shivering.

I would drive a long time, I knew. The car warmed up, and the rain was strong and gray on the neighborhood streets. Though I was younger than I had been, I felt much older; and in the future, we would all become unimaginably older, diminished, a thought that was hard to bear. The perimeters beyond my aunt and uncle's home were gauzy, and I could not think why. I turned and saw Madja sitting beside me.

"You heinous bitch," she said calmly. Her teeth glowed fluorescently in the rain-colored windshield, and I knew she had the strength to kill me.

"Madja," I tried to say.

"Some things are not forgivable, believe me," Madja said.

I don't remember leaving the car, or speaking to her, and I don't know what happened to the fluffy white bird who clung to the seat.

Much later, when I was still compromised every day, I learned that, through Madja, new children had been born into the family, two beautiful, white-haired children who, for many years, I believed were nearly mine. They might grow to understand themselves someday. I miss them all the time.

Milk Boy

EVERYONE CALLED HIM 'Milk Boy' because he was just like milk: thin, rushing everywhere, tinged with blue; he poured himself all around because he needed to; he was nervous and jiggled all day just like a happy little clown, and as a matter of fact, he was a clown, laughing all his life, compromising himself, jerking upon the office floor. But that was just him, this charming Milk Boy who hurtled through the kitchenette to cover up everything with his arms and hands, or any part of himself he could reasonably move or extend.

Embarrassed and ashamed in such a terrible way, and who knew why? No one, really; he ran on his toes, giggling, sad, making a mess of lunch, spreading the backs of his hands on the floor because to be alive itself was an embarrassment, and he wished everyone on earth to forget what they could.

Jumping up because he was simply an active, successful employee, record-keeper, and man, allergic to plants, busy at all times; he raced through the lot to his outsized car, which bloated him along the road home. There, he ran through the hallway to the mirrored door, too touchy to swallow right now or fully speak, let alone to eat a healthful meal of beef, too ashamed to find his gaze, to peek inquiringly into the crevices of his own eyes; and naturally, this charming man was panicked as a rule, though in the future he would certainly own a home and comfortably travel the globe too; but for now, each day was an utter jumble and mess; he could not sleep, but that was just life for this poor, roundabout, clowning, woozy man who, wherever he was, lay embarrassed to death.

He drove to work high across the Eads Bridge, with a little laxative each morning for courage; and he was over-fragile, which never bodes well for office work. He might not last long in life, he knew in the back of his heart. He never had been shown his own strength. But he was too busy all the time to try to understand or calm himself down, for right now he was learning to walk on his hands and juggle on weekends; blazing, leaping through the years, he was jaunty enough to convince himself, making his co-workers laugh, and to suffer was so different from what we ever had imagined.

If only he were a hellion, but he was not. Music made him fall because it was too strong. Once, in the facilities room, he told a colleague he had been born insane, but that it had cleared up. Now gasping, lean, running in long strides toward the elevator door, skidding there, shame the natural color of his hair, he saw his boss Moody Andrews waiting too, so silent, gruff—perhaps it was a problem with bloating or numbness. Then Moody told Milk Boy, woolen-voiced, direct, "I doubt this position is going to work out."

Mightn't anyone feel embarrassed all the time just from being awake or alive, embarrassed, too, at having survived? Milk Boy, all sudden starts and stops, was ashamed by meaning, most of all, and feared ideas of strength; weren't his legs growing blue? Wasn't he a funny young man, controllable, and so for some girls, cute? Thin as floss, but, in his mind, uncomfortably huge; he could not bear the thought of tales or logs; he always slept poorly, incapable of arousing each morning at an appropriate time, and he never dreamed in pictures.

As the elevator doors opened, he looked down into the metal crack: a rushing, roiling stream lay below. Turning around, he saw his parents, each named Glenn, each enormous, each wearing a plush white robe, and as Milk Boy waved, the elevator doors closed.

To be daring and strong and guileless is best, but he knew he was nowhere near that. The elevator rose. He pressed his chest on his newspaper, rubbing, sliding against the rail, hollering in pleasure or relief; who in the world can explain what this is? "No," he yelled, "I will never say anything dumb again," as Moody, watching from the corner of the elevator, suddenly grew tender, it seemed, smiling damply, pulling his collar, squeezing his boxed drink.

The doors opened on the second floor; there was so much to want. Moody beckoned, "Come to my desk!" as Milk Boy stalled and sweated along the elevator's walls; if he wanted, he could run and run, fast as a dog; and he would be all right sometimes, as when his mother had tucked him in for an hour each night; age twenty-seven or forty-nine, it is so easy for people to tie themselves down; can you imagine, in older age, finally growing calm, knowing, and warm? Then nothing will hurt us again, we think, but we are wrong.

And You Are?

IN 1999, WHEN many people said that a crisis might be, but that it might not be, Janice-Katie took some prescription pills and felt a bit better. She knew life had its rough, even intolerable, side, for example, bugs and weeds, and so during this early period of her adulthood, she turned to good, exciting activities, such as weekly movies. In this way, life's tone was more upbeat, as her friends remarked outside the cinema ticket booth. The good side of life was simply better, Janice-Katie told them, though there were sides to life that were neither good nor bad; there were sides that were both, too; there was yet another side that no one could seem to express, and though there should have been no further sides to life, unfortunately, there were.

Janice-Katie went out each day, as she felt she should. In adherence to her entire self-conception, she carried herself as if in need of coddling. She liked to touch her upper arms and frequently smoothed her own neck. Once, near the entrance to the town dry cleaners, she saw someone, it was a woman leaning on a peeled stick. The woman walked slow. Janice-Katie stared. Though it was autumn, a honeysuckle vine had grown onto the pavement; it lay near her ankles, blossoms fused to the stems and ready for life in a terrible way, as far as Janice-Katie could divine.

The woman with the stick advanced. Janice-Katie leaned casually against the store window, her mind fiercely focused, proteinous blood rinsing through her ears, and suddenly, she recalled that, long ago, the woman had been her baby-sitter.

"I am Mrs. Beck," said the older woman uncertainly, throat moving. She stared at Janice-Katie. "And you are…?"

Janice-Katie laughed, as if carefree. She said, "I am Janice-Depressive, you know, like 'manic-depressive'?"

Mrs. Beck frowned.

Years before, Mrs. Beck had come one weekend to care for Janice-Katie. She brought a gift of nuts and a luxuriant blue crème rinse for the hair. The woman led the girl to sit beneath a tree; there, using a flap of green cloth, she taught Janice-Katie the catch stitch, the loop stitch, and how to lower a hem. With the bright sun slanting, Janice-Katie eventually fell asleep, the sewing implements in her lap. When she woke, grasping at the needles, sensing she was nowhere, the tree's shirred leaves hissing in the wind, she asked Mrs. Beck a question about dying.

"Everybody dies," the baby-sitter said authoritatively. "They turn into white crumbs and dust. You and I have some time before we stop being ourselves, though. Yet not too long—you'll see, the time will pass like nothing." At this remark, Janice-Katie lay back, blinking, wishing to pool her physical energy with someone else's.

Another day, lounging in lawn chairs, she and Mrs. Beck drank lemonade with a heightened, delicious, sour taste; Janice-Katie tried to convince the older woman that the sun is the size of a person's hand. Mrs. Beck smiled then, threading a fine needle, appearing not to believe this. The tall house beside them threw an outsized shadow onto the brightly-lit ground. Mrs. Beck said sharply, "What do you think you are doing?" as Janice-Katie reached for a garden flower. Then hurt swam up through the fabric of her dress, blurring its pattern as she stared.

Now, in front of the town dry cleaners, looking at the older woman's gray coat sleeve, Janice-Katie remembered her young, unsuspecting self, and had no feeling to cry.

Mrs. Beck's tidy beige cap looked at odds with the worn stick. She said, "I suppose everything has a purpose. Even a little chip broken off from a red checker"—she pointed with her black shoe-toe on the ground—"has some purpose, doesn't it?"

"What the hell are you talking about?" said Janice-Katie.

"Not that I know its purpose. But surely someone does. The thought of it makes me feel a little better than usual. Then—thank goodness!—I don't need to ask the question 'Why?'" Mrs. Beck kicked the chip away and seemed to steady herself. "So don't you worry, young lady. You'll soon discover your purpose in life!" She began to stroll away.

Janice-Katie felt a surge of lavish anger through her body, powerful in its nerve-eating properties. "Don't you patronize me! And don't call me 'young lady!' You'll call me by my name," she hollered.

The woman turned around. "I don't know your name."

"The problem is that I told you my name a minute ago, but you just don't listen!"

"What you said was not a name," said Mrs. Beck. "It was nonsense. I gave you the benefit of the doubt by ignoring it and now you have forfeited everything," she finished, walking down the block, past the shops, now all closed for the day.

That evening, Janice-Katie stood in her living room. The afternoon's incident did not bother her, because she had a persona. She felt great. Stout and in her fifties, she had a hatred of twilight. Janice-Katie ordered a pizza. The pizza was sour. Yet after dinner she stood on the porch, able to watch the night sky and its high, steam-white clouds, fantastically swift, with enjoyment.

"I am strong," she told herself in a whisper. "My bones seem a solid, unified piece, but they are not! Because of the joints, I guess. Still, I am whole," she emphasized, also aware of an odor, perhaps from some fundamental food such as warm eggs, bread, or milk, drifting across a neighbor's lawn.

Night would go on for six hours more, she knew. The starlight she saw had begun in the past, streaming through the supposedly infinite sky, marking time as clocks. Janice-Katie touched the screen door. She was not near the beginning of her life, nor close to the markers of its end. With its white façade, her house sat unbolted to the earth that tumbled. She went inside and sat on the sofa for a long time, then phoned Mrs. Beck.

2

After some small talk on the phone, Janice-Katie found herself laughing in warm amusement at something Mrs. Beck said. Then older woman queried: "Why is your face so wide?"

"I have a moon face, is all," Janice-Katie stated plainly; "it's an overly wide face due to the side-effects of my stomach medicine. I have lifelong acne, too," she added defensively. "I already know that acne is more or less a written statement about my feelings toward myself, so don't bother harping on it."

She clenched her jaw, but, to Janice-Katie's surprise, Mrs. Beck dropped the topic. The remainder of the conversation was light and easy, and the two women arranged to meet the following day.

Janice-Katie did not like her body to get wet early in the morning. Neither did she care for soap foam. So the next day before dressing, she sprinkled a dry shampoo in her hair, calmly brushing this powder away, proud of her own small ways of keeping clean and comfortable. She then walked to the local lunch house, small feet jerking across the dining room's whorl-patterned carpeting, and cried a friendly hello to Mrs. Beck and the other ladies present.

Holding her tray, moving through the line to purchase corn and tea, Janice-Katie felt her stomach ticking with dread due to Mrs. Beck's strong personality. She was nervous, but managed to sit and joke with Mrs. Beck about the comical sloshing of the tea mugs; she grew more relaxed as the two shared a joke and laughed together about a well-known neighborhood raccoon. Then the two women decided, using a few brief, blunt words, to become long-term partners and com-panions.

They walked downtown together in silence, heading toward the nearest hardware store. Janice-Katie felt the weight of commitment upon her. She imagined Mrs. Beck would move into her home irreversibly, bringing with her a good deal of worn, yellowed furniture, presenting herself constantly for conversation. Janice-Katie felt sick. Nevertheless, slitting her eyes, she smiled, and told herself she must be good-natured. She stated uneasily, "Don't put all your chickens in one basket!"

"Believe me, I wouldn't," Mrs. Beck grumped. "Besides, I dislike both chicken and eggs."

"I like any mild meal," Janice-Katie remarked. "What I don't like is outer space," she said, pointing above her head.

"I'll bear it in mind," said Mrs. Beck.

The pair commenced in the usual ways, working together on domestic projects and growing angry over trivial matters in order to avoid closeness.

Janice-Katie, in the full midst of her life, careful on the flooded ground, sometimes ambled through her yard, checking for weeds or garbage in the thin grass along the house's foundation. At times, she enjoyed walking down the block. From the lawn of the college a short distance away, her house on River Street looked very little and alone and seemed to float above the road.

3

Mrs. Beck stood near the mantle, concerned. "Oh, I feel so swollen with something," she said, and went to the sofa, hands first.

"Cripes," said Janice-Katie. She guided Mrs. Beck to the guest room, lowering her, face-up, onto a bed, though Mrs. Beck was capable of lying down by herself.

The older woman looked at the window and its broad casement. "I hate evening, it is something like dying," she said, palms in the air.

"You are so dramatic, Irene." After a minute she returned to the kitchen. Over time, the former baby-sitter seemed to have come under attack from several sharp maladies that had no names— not yet. She had problems with breathing. For this, she was scheduled to be evaluated in the next month at a nearby famous, though smallish, hospital devoted entirely to the lungs.

The next problem seemed to reside in Mrs. Beck's imagination. She perceived things that were not true. She believed, for example, that Janice-Katie had thrown away her shoes, and that the mailman was trying to follow her on weekends.

"I did nothing to your shoes," Janice-Katie responded dully, once, at midnight, standing between Mrs. Beck's accusing stare and a wooden clock. The older woman then stated that her own nose and breath were diseased.

Distantly, Janice-Katie wished she could bring Mrs. Beck some happiness, at least in the way adults can stir one another briefly from time to time, despite the propinquity of the outer world. But, she thought now, dragging a skillet off the stove, Mrs. Beck could not magically be made happy or well.

She returned to the bedroom's doorjamb, waiting for further remarks from Mrs. Beck.

"Thank goodness my mother died," Mrs. Beck said into the air worriedly. "She would have been so puzzled by my life! By my lack of accomplishments." The TV flickered in the dark room. "You see, I just want to get settled on who I am."

"Irene, isn't it a tad late for that?"

"It's never too late to grow!" Mrs. Beck said. "Haven't you grown? Even in the past few weeks?"

Janice-Katie snorted. She took care of everything now, saw to all Mrs. Beck's home needs. Her own daily routine was drab, Janice-Katie felt. But inside the constraints of work and chores and Mrs. Beck's near-complete dependence, she sometimes sensed a fluorescence in the air around her, a possibility. She breathed it in. It was a type of freedom, she supposed.

She returned to the room, carrying a little square blanket for Mrs. Beck, who lay back, resting. Reaching into her dress pocket, Janice-Katie withdrew a cigarette.

"If I turn away to a private world of my own," Mrs. Beck said, "will I still be part of the common world?" Janice-Katie did not feel like giving Mrs. Beck the satisfaction of a reply. The older woman looked to the wall, groaning lightly, asking for a hairbrush, complaining that her nose hurt.

Receding toward the kitchen storage area, private and alone, Janice-Katie inhaled, feeling wonderfully alive and strong. She was pleased that she needed so little medicine these days. At this point, in comparison to others, her body certainly might be the leanest, possibly most well-functioning body on the block and the neighborhood, possibly in the entire town. Even if that were not perfectly, factually true, it also did not seem incorrect, insofar as Janice-Katie was absolutely unique. Now it seemed as if her own future infirmity, traveling toward her like an old man on a long, barely visible road, might vanish. It might be reabsorbed into the atmosphere or the road itself, or it might be destroyed by something surprising.

"I can always prove myself by getting a job!" Mrs. Beck broke out from the back of the house.

Soon Janice-Katie would attend to the chore of washing and stretching all of Mrs. Beck's trousers, for, day by day, the woman's legs were swelling with water or some other substance. She thought she heard Mrs. Beck calling again.

4

A few months later, Mrs. Beck returned home. She had been away for four days. "Hello!" Janice-Katie said, eyes smiling, and shut the door. Mrs. Beck set down her leaden suitcase. She had found a job as a mobile seamstress for a busy advertising company whose employees made presentations at conventions. However, she felt that the job might not be stimulating enough for her.

Mrs. Beck sat in a straight chair. She was tired. During her absence, she and Janice-Katie had exchanged a few letters through the mail.

"Are you well?" said Janice-Katie.

"Yes, except for my breathing," Mrs. Beck answered. After the experience at the hospital, her inspiratory breaths had become even more jagged and difficult. However, she often had enough breath for strenuous activities; a few days before, she had hauled several heavy wastepaper baskets full of needles and ugly telephones away from her station at work.

"I didn't speak to anyone on the train," she told Janice-Katie. "It's too weakening."

"There's no need to talk on a train," said the younger woman.

Mrs. Beck looked at the living room window, lowered her head, and slept. When she woke, she was near-certain it was nighttime. But it could also have been daytime, for the dank-looking sky could have belonged to either. She glanced around, for Janice-Katie would know the current time down to the millisecond. Janice-Katie had that type of wristwatch.

She was sitting in the semi-darkness, holding a cup of odorous tea. "Stop asking questions," Janice-Katie said, refusing to tell Mrs. Beck the time, perhaps from spite. "It's tiresome," she went on, adding in murmured tones that she was not interested in milliseconds, or in the precise nature of time. Then Mrs. Beck's loneliness was thin as the tears covering her eyes, which she blinked back while watching the quiet street with its irregularly shaped lawns and the few messy, blowing trees that no one bothered pruning. She noted the thick, dusty edge of the beige window curtain, comforting in its stillness.

On a snowy afternoon long before, a schoolteacher, in the midst of the classroom's raucous noise, had explained that day and night were opposite in nature. The teacher, Miss Helen Perkins, had been young and precocious, with apple-ish cheeks, and Mrs. Beck had admired her. Once, she even had felt wounded enough by the coarse goings-on of high school to go sit in the teacher's lap for the duration of a film-strip.

"Dammit, they're the same!" Mrs. Beck said now, shifting in her chair.

"What's the same?" answered Janice-Katie.

"Day and night!" she yelled. "God, they're not opposites! That's unbelievably stupid. They are the two sides of the same thing—our world. Miss Perkins lied about it."

"Perkins? She wasn't a liar," said Janice-Katie. She had known Miss Perkins, too, after the teacher had become a quiet retiree living on a hill separate from downtown, yet linked to it by a rock road. "I think she loved whatever was true. She was pure."

"She was ignorant!" Mrs. Beck cried.

"Irene, you are having a spell," Janice-Katie said dully.

"She never kept up with the current thinking. She schemed. She was trying to bring me down into shame— others too! The maintenance man!"

And now Janice-Katie was ushering her to the sofa, unfolding the blanket, telling her to rest, though her mind would not rest. It was unbearable to think Miss Perkins had deliberately gypped her out of a broader education, and more. Trying to inhale, she felt a deep, familiar thirst for air. But relief did not really come from breathing, after all; it came from the release of asking long-impacted questions and from receiving satisfying answers.

Mrs. Beck struggled to sit up. "Janice-Katie, in the letter I wrote you last week—"

"What about it?" Janice-Katie's palms pressed the top of an armchair.

"In the letter, do you remember, I made a joke about mayonnaise? Then I wrote the words 'ha-ha—'"

"I remember."

"In your reply, you made your own joke—about barricading the house—and you also wrote 'ha-ha.'"

"So?"

"Did you write 'ha-ha' because I wrote 'ha-ha'?"

"Oh, will you stop it?!" Janice-Katie sank onto the window sill.

"For hell's sake, this is important! How much do we influence one another? Does my mind suggest things to your mind? If I had never written 'ha-ha,' would you have written 'ha-ha'?

Janice-Katie said heavily, "I don't remember saying 'ha-ha."

"You didn't say 'ha-ha,' you wrote 'ha-ha.' Why say you said it when you wrote it? Now, try to remember, if you care about me or about life at all!"

"Irene, something's gone wrong with you."

"No, no—you're the one who's uncooperative."

"Try to sleep."

"In the middle of the day? Or is it night, and you're just not telling me? Do you want me to sleep so you can be rid of me, or because you think I'm sick? Answer the questions!"

"Yes—yes to all of that." Janice-Katie picked at a hang nail.

Mrs. Beck burst out, "It can't be 'yes' to each! Now, please—I won't be able to sleep until you answer the question about 'ha-ha.'"

"Well, you're going to have to try."

Mrs. Beck smacked her hands together in anger. Janice-Katie had become too stubborn or dull to answer incisive, even wonderful questions that could bring clarity to life's tangled moments. They grew painful if left unanswered. But Janice-Katie did not care, and seemed content to live as if beneath a shroud. It was left up to Mrs. Beck to scan time's surfaces and past occurrences and make certain things were clear. The responsibility of asking questions was heavy, she realized, drawing up her legs, extending them on the sofa.

A moment later, Janice-Katie was asking a question of her own: "Don't you remember a few weeks ago when I asked you if we could stop arguing for good?"

Mrs. Beck remembered vaguely, and felt a pinching sadness. "Well— I remember the colors of the day." She closed her eyes. "Did I answer only what you wanted to hear? Or was the answer part of my own mind?"

While resting, Mrs. Beck began planning a long, meandering walk that would involve leaving the house within moments, alone. She would take her time, forcing Janice-Katie to wonder her whereabouts. Winding along the flat, bare pathways of a nearby park, her mind would relax, as now. She would not return to her sewing job in the next week, she knew, because of the questions that rose in her mind like sprays of oxygen. Did the mind these days count as part of the body? In the park, she would approach strangers and freely ask any questions that were necessary to ask. The people in the park would be polite, wearing tidy, well-made caps and coats; they would answer cheerfully. She could choose any one of them to play checkers with her on the bench, and each conversation would go just as she imagined.

Mrs. Beck began to doze again. She would not go for a walk today, she realized. It was unclear to her if she spoke her thoughts aloud: "Do all people who are sleeping contribute to the world, and help it? Oh, I so hope the answer is yes."

5

The next day, Mrs. Beck emerged from a nap.

Janice-Katie was standing beside her bed, watching. "Let's go out for a snack," she said. "That may distract you from your cares."

"Snack?" Mrs. Beck sounded worried, as if the word were a euphemism for something dire.

"We can walk to the stadium café."

"But— can stadium food be good for us?" Mrs. Beck quavered, though she rose hurriedly, sliding her feet into shoes, finding her coat, wrapping it around her.

"We'll see Bill Orange, no doubt," said Janice-Katie, as the pair headed through the gray streets and across an empty intersection. The sports complex sat on the far side of the college lawn.

"Who?"

"You know, the snack-bar man. He's not bad."

"He *is* bad!" Mrs. Beck said. "He's blunt. I don't want to see Bill Orange or anyone like that today, because I'm setting out to keep a clear mind and feel better."

"You'll cheer up as soon as you see him."

"He's berserk."

"Your view of normal is very narrow," Janice-Katie said as the two walked onward, growing quiet, though Mrs. Beck moaned, running a finger through her hair and upon her sleeves and collar, as if searching for a warm seam.

The pair entered the stadium area, with its open amusement section and metal picnic tables. No game was held on this day. So the place was empty, and the low-lying snack trailer was open, as nearly always. Though the weather was cool, a bright yellow insect lamp hung beneath the trailer's canopy. A man in an apron, standing beside the grill, regarded the women with lively eyes. A poster on the trailer window depicted a crock of white soup and a gabled European chalet.

Janice-Katie greeted him. "Bill, why aren't you wearing a coat?"

"Forget about that," said Bill Orange. "I've got Dutch soup."

Mrs. Beck leaned toward Janice-Katie. "I wouldn't touch the food here," she said.

"Fine by me," said the man, angrily passing a whisk between his palms. After a moment, he added: "Ever been to Holland?"

Mrs. Beck stared at him. "I hate traveling. What a shame, to do that with yourself."

"Hush," said Janice-Katie, scanning the plastic menu on the wall. "You know, I'd like to try something cool and watery!"

The man did not respond. "I always train myself to eat and experience what's new," he said, eyeing Mrs. Beck. "That strengthens me for new challenges. Why don't you try doing that?"

"You'll not tell me how to live," she said.

"Well, I'm setting out to do exciting things, huge things. And some awful things," Bill Orange grinned. "You really can't imagine."

"What?" Mrs. Beck's voice grew anxious. "Why did you say 'exciting,' and then the word 'awful'? What were you thinking about? You don't mean hobbies— do you feel hobbies are boring, a form of mental death?

Are you talking about force-feeding someone in your basement? That couldn't be."

"Shut up, Lady, or I'll call the police," Bill Orange said crossly over his shoulder, now tapping some small, soft-looking cubes of food into a bowl of flour.

"But those are all good questions!"

"Listen," the man said, setting a knuckle on the counter. "Get out of here."

"You're the one who used the word 'awful!'" Mrs. Beck cried. She glanced at Janice-Katie, who continued to peruse the menu.

"Never mind all that, Beck," said Janice-Katie. "I'll have something cold," she repeated.

The man wiped two fingers on his apron sash. "Fine. But on a chilly day like this?"

"Oh," Janice-Katie said, "I often want cool food. It doesn't mean anything about me or my personality, though. Sometimes I wish they'd invent a machine that would chill meals instantly," she went on, gesturing at the convection oven with its loud, blowing sound. "Like that, only cold. You'd put the food in, and after one minute, it would be icy and delicious!"

"You mean a refrigerator, dammit," said Mrs. Beck, now watching tersely at a distance, her feet in a puddle of tin-colored rainwater.

"No, not a refrigerator!" said Bill Orange. "Use your head! When I was young, you'd meet all kinds of people who'd come up to this counter and could really think clearly, and boy, could they reason! Here now: a refrigerator cools food slowly!"

"And a freezer?" said Mrs. Beck, a challenge in her voice.

Bill Orange held up a sharp, warning finger to Mrs. Beck, staring widely at her, shaking his head. Then he turned to Janice-Katie.

"It's funny, you used to act different with her— shyer," he said, nodding toward Mrs. Beck.

The man set food onto plates. "Here are your sandwiches, Girls," he said. "But—" He turned toward the deep hollow of a wooden cabinet, his voice falling. "Shoot. I'm out of fancy toothpicks. There's no mustard, either."

The man grew quiet as he spooned lettuce and a beige cream over the sandwiches. He set the lunch plates on a high, floury shelf. After a few minutes, sitting on a stool, he asked: "How in hell's name did that happen?"

"No one can eat until this thing is sorted out," he said heavily. "Now, it's acceptable to forgo toothpicks; it's done frequently. But mustard... that's different." He put a hand to his temple, and then withdrew it so quickly that the movement nearly looked like a salute.

"I want both of you to head over to the supply room right now and fetch the mustard."

"Ridiculous," said Mrs. Beck.

"No— you go, you both go!" Bill Orange sounded strained. His face shone with sweat, and he seemed more worried than he could aptly express. "It'll be damned easy for you to get it. You see, I can't do it, and I'm not going to! I have troubles I'm not going to discuss right now. So you both will just go and get the mustard. Besides, I've got no time to go—I'm too far behind in terms of slaw."

"You know, I'm not convinced you're not a huge liar," said Mrs. Beck.

"Go on to the supply room now, the both of you!" the man burst out hotly, jumping up. He flung a hand in the direction of the stadium, indicating a certain section of bleachers on the far side. "You'll see the door all right, just underneath those seats...it's unlocked! Here now, when tomorrow comes, you won't remember that you even went to the supply room! Go on, go on, fetch a few darned bottles of mustard," he finished weakly.

Leaning with his arm over the counter, the man added that it would be next to impossible to miss the supply room door, because it was so brightly painted, but mostly because, on the wall directly beside it, a very small drinking fountain recently had been mounted, possibly for children.

"Bill," Janice-Katie said hesitantly. "You know, they say everyone has problems. I didn't think you did, though. I never thought much about you at all."

"Ah," he said sullenly, closing a lid on some butter.

"You can't go to the supply room, I guess, because you have pain moving your body around— your legs," she suggested.

"It's got nothing to do with that!" Bill Orange yelled.

"Oh. Then is it because you have personal fears about leaving this trailer, or some kind of superstition?"

"Shut up!"

Janice-Katie tightened her coat cheerfully around her and took Mrs. Beck's arm, beginning to walk toward the stadium. "Don't worry, Bill. We'll get the mustard for you."

"Has this world gone nuts?" cried Mrs. Beck. "I'm not going to a supply room! Oh, I knew it was a mistake to come here." She made as if to pull away from Janice-Katie, who outpowered her.

"Don't make a scene about an errand," said Janice-Katie.

"Goodbye!" Bill Orange called softly.

"Why in grief's name do you think he is so wonderful?" Mrs. Beck fumed as they walked.

Janice-Katie did not answer.

She kept a grip on Mrs. Beck, pulling, steering the way, while Mrs. Beck, aggravated, pushed Janice-Katie. Moving fast, the two breathed harder, passing through the open stadium gate and breaking into the light and air of the field. The clouds had cleared, and the upper ring of the enormous, empty stadium focused the entire sky against the sun.

Janice-Katie looked up. A lost bat flew across the bleachers, flapping and diving out of sight so quickly it seemed possible that it had not flown at all.

She let go of Mrs. Beck's arm, and in an awkward, hobbling manner, began to walk even more quickly; then she began to run. The older woman yelled once, an unclear syllable, and started running too, keeping pace slightly behind Janice-Katie, her dark coat flapping. Soon both the women found their way into light, steady, if lilting gaits, and then Janice-Katie pushed forward, gaining a good deal of speed.

"I enjoy the running!" Mrs. Beck cried, catching up, then falling behind slightly again. She ran lumberingly, swinging her arms in overlarge movements, and she listed off somewhat diagonally. Mrs. Beck's speed seemed to issue from the force and momentum of her moving weight, while Janice-Katie felt her own quickness came from the unrelenting, rapidly skittering movements of her feet and legs.

Surprised at the running, which seemed to have begun somewhat outside her mind or will, Janice-Katie expelled a laugh—a brief, birdish noise. The spongy ground, she felt, curtailed her pace, but she tried to overcome this and in stretching her heels, managed to go even faster. Her gait was now oddly forward-leaning, though she sensed this helped control the run. She looked down to her black, slipper-style shoes, judging their thin soles to be an asset. She was aware of the smallness of her feet and the force of her weight beating into them.

"The mustard will be there," she told herself.

The run was long. Janice-Katie felt it was occurring slowly, a subtle eternity. She settled into strong, regular breaths. The wind dragged in her ears as she moved; the stadium floated past. Mrs. Beck pulled a tissue from her pocket and, barreling along, blew her nose and wiped wind-induced tears from her face.

Janice-Katie thought: "I am in a private world, standing against her private world. But it is harmonious."

Much of her life's time had passed. But some of it was still stored, as if within a vaulted bank. Janice-Katie's legs churned alongside Mrs. Beck's flying, churning legs, and a spot of burning white—the sun—held constant as they passed through the field. It was easy.

Sausage

A FACTORY OF upside-down bicycles, this was the way to make sausages, pedaling so quickly with my hands, my feet; never a thought for stopping, unable to know if I was sitting or standing; unaware if the daytime was starting or ending—

In those days, my every muscle was willing; the meat was all ready, well ground, as if chewed; I churned wild circles, miles of bloody brown sausage accumulating beneath my wheels; perhaps I lagged; I was worried, filled with shame; but wasn't my work earnest? Wouldn't I produce to the heavens? My limbs were adept, for squeezing forth sausage in regular shapes, and my fingers strong, too, for each night, very late, I sewed all the skins shut with a heavy black thread, knotting it twice to keep everything in—

The Warder entered: huge, circling, judging our production, the condition of our bodies. Yes, I nodded, in answer to everything he said, while sensing, as ever, that I had done something wrong; indeed, the Warder's very presence implied that this was so. He laughed uproariously, for a reason I could not discern; then, in a sudden rage, boomed that our legs were pathetic, weak, weaker than rags; they must be oiled, strengthened, the muscles stretched; he stooped then, massaging my calf with a thick handful of fat, and put his lips to my ear, whispering, "There is a strong chance that this ointment will not help you at all. And I worry, you see, for when your failure occurs, it is my failure too; I depend on you; so in a sense, does the entire nation; we need sausage; it is now a staple; so, don't suddenly move, or draw attention to yourself; in other words, be true, even-keeled—display high spirits! Don't let your mind stray. Have you ever seen me lose my temper?"

He left, thumping shut the barn door (these buildings were solid, hand-built decades before, twenty stories wide and tall); churning wildly, I breathed for more sausage, ashamed that my attention ever had wandered; how could it have, with our work being so vitally important?

Sweating heavily at my station, I grew worried again, frightened of failure, and full of shame; then suddenly, from sheer nervousness, I pushed forth monstrously, producing more sausage than in the entire hour previous; and production was relief, as the Warder always had said; and he was right, too. Drenched, exhausted, emptied of strength, I decided that I must immediately change, and learn to selflessly give—of myself, and my body, as if giving a gift.

That year we had seen record production, the ninety of us issuing more sausage per day than ever had been achieved; our numbers were steady— incredible numbers, rising daily, so that it became no longer possible for the management to tabulate our work in the usual way; so newer, higher numbers were found to express our rates, though these numbers themselves quickly became outmoded, outpaced; then, even higher, more superlative symbols were employed, and in approaching the final horizon of numbers, the barrier to infinity, we grew giddy, as if on a ride; administrators worried; precise counts were lost; secret meetings were planned, military exercises; yet through it all, an enormous excitement, for, with our bodies, we had produced such fantastic amounts—with the sheer force of our wills, too, our wishes to be good, and with the help of regular punishments—

The meat was always ready, boiled hard, in vats; the skins lay in rows, clean, stretched; everything in order; nothing was the matter; barring, occasionally, a ripple of emotion—anger or pleasure rolling inside us, as if deep beneath the crust of a mountain—

Our wants were satisfied daily; our mats lay spread in the barn; ten minutes of sleep before each back-to-back shift; to eat, sausage-gruel in huge amounts; to drink, steaming cups of blood, as much as we liked. There was time, too, if we wished, to find one of the confused, blurred critters who wandered these yards, and lead it away for relief in some corner of the dark—

"Good, very tender," said the Warder, having entered, stooping to test the links with his teeth. "Continue," he cried, arms trembly. "Today work for size; tonight, for speed! Achievement, achievement—but I worry that you will not—" then he turned away, dropping his huge, hairy head to his palms, overcome. "My God," he whimpered, "I can't manage my own doubt—"

Alarmed, we pedaled faster, ninety bicycles whirring in place; on my seat, I pushed harder than ever, continual bursts of dampness like storms at the back of my neck; sausage dropped through the rafters, to the floor in gleaming coils. "Ah," groaned the Warder, raising his swimming eyes, "keep going, don't fall behind!"

So I pressed on, dripping a meat-scented sweat, whispering the highest known numbers to myself—

For there was nothing else beyond these walls, only the empty town of Nicholls, and beyond that, the silent, wind-soaked plains of "France"; there were no other nations besides our own, a fact we had learned long before, in youth—

During these weeks of stupendous growth, I became, at certain moments, somewhat cocky, even brash, once slipping from my station, muscles shaking, laughing to myself from sheer tension; I sought a lone, dry corner, swallowing down a piece of beer-soaked bread (having stolen it shamelessly from a nearby trough—an act which, eventually, would weigh gravely on my list of wrongs). I grew thoughtful, serious, legs apart, powerful, thick, and resembled, in these moments, as it happened, the Warder, bellowing tremendously; then embarrassed, I struck myself with the back of my fist. Suddenly, I heard a whisper spurt through the air, landing in my ear, as if mad to get home; the words were hard and clear. They told me to take charge, as it were, and stop suffering needlessly because of my work. A plan came miraculously to me then: I would assume responsibility for all the mistakes, foibles, and wrongdoings of another sausage-maker, now dead.

I had not known this man, but I would soon set out to possess all his wrongs: in this way, I saw, my own guilts would be obscured; I would atone for him publicly, thereby winning respect from the management; I would live freely then, never again burdened by the weight of my actions or their consequences.

Early the next morning, I went to ask permission, duly, officially, before a panel of porcine judges assembled in the lower barn (chairs stacked high against the rear wall, and stored between each, a thick layer of winter sausage fully encrusted by salt and meant to nourish the highest of the management, keep them warm against the deadly cold). I was vocal; I expressed myself clearly; I wanted to possess the dead man's wrongs and repent for him, since I was so exemplary—

With the banging of a gavel, they assented, scarcely looking up; it was decided; I was to live the rest of my life atoning for the dead one's wrongs; it was official; now, at every turn, I would be enfolded by his innumerable ill deeds, with my own movements free from suspicion, for the first time in my existence—

Such relief! All my life, I had needed this. Exuberant, I stepped up to embrace the administrators, judges, and even the mayor, who briefly had stepped in. Though in clasping him, my lips brushing his scented beard, I realized that he was devoid—not numb and overfed, as with diplomats, nor brainwashed, as by religion—but empty, outrageously blank of any mental content or register, resembling, even faintly, a birth monster.

And then, from sheer excitement, he mewled, looking to the ceilings, bobbing his head, and everyone laughed, for he was a docile, well-loved man, and filled his post perfectly, I had heard.

Giddy, I raced toward my station, springing past stalls, careering through aisles, sluice gates, pulling up my pants, invigorated, thrilled by the thought of acquiring the dead one's wrongs, and then, by chance, I passed his pale body in the dim hall, where, naked like others, it was strapped against the wall, embalmed, on display, completely shaven, head dropped down, for he had simply weakened, then died of work, a crime under jurisdiction of both factory and state. Diagrams and arrows, supplemented by a brief text, were printed on his flaccid torso to explain exactly how the veins of his heart had burst and collapsed—this occurrence had been entirely due to his own problems: poor habits and disorganization, most probably, it read. Secured in a bottle to his left lay the heart itself, ravaged bloody roots springing from its top. All had been his fault, only his, the tract read, since he had been unable to manage his time and work, and misfortunes like these were just part of life and could happen to anyone, at any time. Still, this man's case was fairly rare, the text said, a fact that made everyone thankful and glad; and soon, it finished, there would be a celebration for all living employees who were wonderful with detail, and, in general, good; so, as a rule, deaths like these would scarcely occur if we worked dependably and always produced as much as we could.

Having run all the way, I arrived at my station, nearly forgetting who I was, producing sausage to such delirium, yet luckier than most, I felt, and surely not dead, and perhaps, I dared hope, the best worker in the place, since I was so wholesome, full of energy, and, starting today, so completely without wrongdoing that even I was astounded. Then, somehow, that night, I began to doubt. I checked the list I kept beneath my mat: indeed, I had committed no outstandingly wrong acts, except for the minor infraction of the bread, and I could explain this by saying I had been seeking to emulate the Warder, and had tried to gain weight; surely I would not be punished for eating, I decided; so for now I was safe.

Throwing my head back, hooting with relish, raising a rough, corrugated stick we often used to show purpose and excitement, I began to pedal backward (a trick we knew for making sausages fancier, bloodier, less congealed, stronger in color). I was free; life was different, my luck would hold because of the dead one's deeds. No more burden or remorse; my wheels raced steadily, while below, piglets scrambled across the floors in packs; surely I was good, and produced properly at all moments—this being the pride and requirement of our factory and nation. All was fine, I reassured myself, combing my hair, rearranging my smock, forking, when no one was looking, steaming heaps of meat into my mouth—

My neighbor to one side, an elder, was wheezing, exhausted as he worked, bathed in a dark, slick sweat. He raised his head, eyes bewildered, and cried out, "Forget the dead one—your scheme is transparent! It's shameful, in fact, this business of racing around as you do, trying to look enthused so you can get away with as much as you can!"

"I did what I had to do," I said calmly. "It was an honest impulse, and I don't have to explain myself. One thing, though, honestly: I feel better and more vigorous than I have in years. Don't repeat this, but I earned my freedom through cunning, and no one else before me has done that—but then, I was never part of the common pack. Why don't you stop being petty, and congratulate me? I no longer live as do you, constricted, worried, and guilty!"

He laughed for a long time, tears streaming down his face. "Your head is in the clouds! No one is here to keep you back or make you feel bad. The guilty are guilty because they do not fit in!" He slid from his station, bent, still laughing, wiping his body with a blue rag.

"How do you know that?" I said, yanked by discomfort.

"Because I have a bigger heart than you," he said, standing there naked, pointing to his own chest, digging the finger in hard as if to break the skin. "I know the truth, for I am clean, appropriate, and have never strayed a day from work. You work for this factory, so why do you behave as if it were your adversary? That will age and ruin you. Instead, just relax; give in to the notion that life is naturally in place. The pressure we feel at work is no plot, no one person's fault. It's just a part of regular life."

I scoffed, but in a sense, the old man was right. He only had been trying to prepare me for the next sequence of events, which began a few moments later, when I received at my station, a strong, sudden message wired from the Manager-in-Absentia, which went like this:

"Just leave it, and let it go. Give yourself the luxury of a few moments' rest, since soon you will want to disappear. Do you fear the surprise of learning you are wrong? I hate to shatter your happiness, for I know you are proud. It was nothing in particular, not even your most recent infraction that brought you into the limelight; it was the accrual of years of your inability to settle down. We will take our time; we will let you know; do you wonder what will happen? Now, repeat the word 'fiasco' over and over, repeat it now, in dialect precisely as is mine, not—I warn you—in parody; repeat it honestly, and with effort, because—and this is God's truth—there is a job now available in the mountain district, and in order to be considered for it, you must successfully be able to reproduce a mountain accent, not just once, but consistently, in a variety of circumstances."

All this, contained in the crumpled message, was followed by a second note relaying that the job in the mountains was still open, though it might soon close, and that this would be an excellent position for anyone with talent, it read, like me, and with the native ability to blend in imperceptibly with anyone or anything.

My neighbor, now back at his station, bathed in rivers of sweat, lunging, straining to make sausage, about to faint, leaned toward me, whispering hoarsely, meat on his breath, "Tear up the message! And let me tell you the most important thing!"

At which point a lean figure entered the barn, rolling the fainted man away, smiling, wiping his hands, clapping them twice, saying, "Can you please stop behaving in ways that belie your unconscious motives?"

"I never do that," I said.

"Oh, God, you do!"

"Who are you?" I said.

"I am Rolf," he answered, "but that doesn't matter. In fact, it's important that you know little about me. But I care about you, and so will say this: in your histrionic taking of the dead man's guilt, you have displayed your troubles as if the workplace were a theatre—very inappropriate, and you don't seem to realize it. Which in itself is important, for it shows us that you cannot see life as it really is, but only as you experience it— including your feelings about me—hesitation and distrust, I believe, and only because my clothes are smart and pressed, which you adolescently perceive as some kind of threat.

"What is taking on the guilt of another? It is hiding your own guilt, and escaping the plain responsibility we carry. Don't worry; I am the sole person who has discussed you with the Manager-in-Absentia. Now, don't pretend; you are not going to walk away; where would you go, in the middle of 'France'? I know a lot about you; for example, your frequent, sudden urges to ingest sleeping tablets—that is a symptom we'll have to address. Well, back to work," he said, "on sausage, and your problems. Begin a resume, too, addressing the question, 'have you ever in your life been humiliated or dismissed?' Because—you know this—in order to groom and promote our men, we managers must have true, exact accounts of everything that's ever happened, grounding present judgments soundly on past circumstances."

He turned and left; my knees collapsed; I was now exposed, much more than before; even the dead man's guilts were no protection against this Rolf. I grabbed myself, beginning to run through the yards, embarrassed to disbelief, for it was true, I loved to sleep, but had such difficulty achieving this. I entered the storage cellars, with piglets galloping, screaming overhead; I bent to examine the hem of my smock, finding a tablet neatly hidden there, and swallowed it, and fell to sleep, dreaming of knives that ran in organized legions, each with a short, distinct, Christian name: Gore, for example; fear saps one's strength like nothing else; waking the next day, I worried about achievement, about never catching up, and about living the rest of my life in the margins, among the ranks of the unproductive. I was stunned, unaccustomed to refuting the likes of Rolf, but instead, all my life, in school and throughout, I had always obeyed clear instructions (or else furtively enacted the precise opposite of these, for which I routinely had been found out and punished). But now I could not think, hating myself and my weaknesses, hating my failed plan to obscure my guilts and faults, hating, for a moment, the entire factory, and our nation—

Then I received, suddenly, a rushed message, delivered to my station by crow; this was due, perhaps, to the lateness of the hour, or the recent shutdown of electricity in patterned on-off intervals—not a gratuitous event, we often were told, but rather playful in spirit, and carried out, in a way, to invite the workers to decipher the codes in such patterns, to strengthen our minds and to keep us alert. The message informed me of a special tax that would be computed relative to the amount of sausage I produced; and after one year, the message said, I would also have a tax upon my legs, and the bicycle I used.

I went wild with fury, blowing out a great wind of screams, clattering through the slaughter area, sweeping entire sets of tiny wrenches from their shelves, stabbing the air, inhaling whole dust clouds; now, the factory would force me to give up what I had earned; loath to do so, shamed still more that I had scarcely any money to be taxed, arms windmilling, hurling clots of mud to the ceilings, I stopped. Yes, of course I would pay the tax, I thought mincingly, but not the precise amount; just a few cents less, or even more, as I chose, only to irritate and disfigure the accounts.

Regardless, I still wanted to achieve, as the Warder had admonished; so did everyone: the managers, and even Rolf. We wanted to work, contribute, and in effect, be good; otherwise, life could grow diffuse and dissolve, and then we would have nothing at all.

Sprinting up ladders, past gristle bags, buckets of swash, plundered mattresses, I aimed for my station, then produced sausage faster than I ever remembered. I jumped down, stuffing barrels full, grabbing the handles, hurrying toward the greeting center, anxious to do well, driven as never before, turning around, going to the bathroom in the middle of the hall, running through the atrium, hands warmly extended to customers who now streamed in from their cars, all of them buying and eating hugely of sausage, voracious, hardworking people, big as houses, cheering at anything, chanting while driving on vacations, nostalgic for times that never existed, bearing sausage away to vehicles and trailers, laughing, whooping, whipping the air three times with their fists, growing impatient, demanding satisfaction. So, running back to my bicycle, I produced just that—sausage, pouring forth at its freshest, to be consumed within moments by unknown persons—

Perhaps I was angry, though most of all, I was deeply ashamed—for myself, and for everything that ever had been, for miscalculating miniscule details of my movements that the Manager-in-Absentia might somehow see, for taking on the guilts of another, trying to lose myself in order to be free, for not having known the notes of the scales, nor the geography of Madeira; ashamed, too, before Rolf, who seemed to know my every thought, who surely ran daily to his flimsy, molding desk to update careful weekly notes. Yet in the future—I only hoped—perhaps he might come fetch me at the abandoned schoolyard where I ran the steep tor to strengthen my limbs, and would call out my name across the field (concerned, paternal, I desperately wished), and "Did you vomit blood?" his coat flapping fiercely in freezing wind—

There was nowhere else to go beyond these quiet streets of Nicholls, beyond the empty plains of "France," no one at all with whom to discuss work, except possibly Rolf, but certainly not with his administrative equal, a man I had once glimpsed while hiding beneath floor planks—a beefy, sluggish bureaucrat, who, slumping at his desk, rasped on the phone all night, "No! I cannot talk to you now!" while feverishly conducting a conversation with himself, purple-faced, trudging in circles around a toilet, saying his name aloud in a power fantasy, drawing huge breaths, expelling joy from his mouth at the idea of commanding dirty creatures down the aisles and to work, soon to have his voice function as would a telephone, connected to every room, and connected, eventually, into the very natures of all people, which would bring everything to satisfaction for him, the administrator with his clannish team of clerks—

The entire team of leaders, minus Rolf, hands folded, eyes moistly beckoning, would call out to me soon, as I stepped onto the wire work floor to begin my shift anew. "Come, come, what is this nonsense? We sympathize, we're friends; we want to understand, so that you are no longer beleaguered by your own tendencies. Never mind the infraction of the bread. But as for the sleeping tablets, we know they were hidden in your smock; we know you use them to leave your body, to become inert; but frankly, in the precise moment that we discovered them, those tablets became ours; that is—the movement is smoothly complex—for us, knowing is the same as a swift, confiscating action; we derived this from an algorithm we compacted until it finished exactly as we liked. All is settled; we have the tablets and you do not. Don't sleep; instead, let's now talk, and examine your mind as it is discussed in texts, the ways you misperceive the world due to your own defensiveness, the way you project feelings about yourself into the world of work. There are so many things you imagine we managers do, each rather unconnected to the truth—do you feel a nervousness inside you that comes from remaining, for years, unchanged? Let's now look at all the shame you've ever endured and collect it together as in a little half-shell, so you can feel it all at once, along with the fallacies to which you cling, and then, perhaps, you will see yourself more clearly and something important can be achieved.

"We will learn why you chose to take on the guilt of another, and why you wanted to be more free, and tried, sometimes, to escape into sleep, with the white tablets you so cunningly ground into powder—as if we could be fooled! As if we would believe they were, perhaps, tooth cleanser?"

Tearing through the yards, I slammed into the cellar, panting, motionless, peering all night through a weephole into the slaughtering barn, waiting for a clear space into which I might run, or for a path into the lower barns where various administrators, standing around, would watch me rocket forward and back as I burst upon myself like a broken bomb—

They had always known I might destruct, for I had always been fully and utterly found out, never mind the dead one and his stupendous wrongs; I had always been entrenched in Nicholls, on the silent plains with nothing beyond.

"Considering everything, you're doing quite well," Rolf said, walking past; "I'd like to talk someday if you're able; we can drink warm water in cups, but for now, don't fuss; back to work, for you've missed far too much, but can make it up if you really push—"

Looking at me, though I was still in the cellar, concealed, Rolf twitched his finger gently, speaking through the hole, "Come out now, it's time to greet the customers, try to get through it; you know the routine well—"

They were packed in their cars, and then they emerged, large men begging for sausage, nearly collapsing as they approached, crying out, "My beliefs are literally part of the land!" One of them pulled me aside, whispering, "Please, before we go back, may I service you just once, upside down, flat on your back; then, holding you still, just once again?"

But all of that was long ago. In the days just before this most astonishing year, we ran from the remotest wood-cracked halls to the placards tacked upon street signs in the town, each of which said, "You are in 'France,'" so take care, don't stray, keep robust; this is the land of enormous plenty. Someday soon, you will get your due, but for now, check yourself daily; just look toward sausage, and the truth." We shattered these messages; now they are forgotten; it is five o'clock on the huge, slanting plaza, and now, crowds have gathered to celebrate, refusing all news that protest is unwarranted—

Still, we do not know who or what is victorious, or if that is even the pertinent question; I am not who I once was; kiosk windows fall open, knots of people expand, newsgirls shout, "It is nine o'clock, and due to a rather global pressure, a motion has been passed for the work day to be called off! The popular forces demand it; all manner of change will be discussed; we will wait, then decide our course, but for now, there is everything to do and see; go to your windows; didn't know it? Look at all the people who are willing to join us—"

This was our nation, the true nation, after all; we thought we had no home, but in fact, we do; the commotion will continue; push your stockings down, loosen your underclothes and belt; in the War of Independence, doors on the plaza opened, and a thousand dark-cloaked bicycle riders emerged, legs outstretched, heading for the clock tower, gliding as if upon amber, with an exalted whisper on everyone's brain, unique and indescribable, like the birth of each new child: "Here are our desires; here are still more, such as we know." We sensed profound relief when our voices' true sounds were heard; a great, healthful confusion has arisen; here is what we wish for; here is what we never had; by dawn, we will have unraveled the worst and rearranged the rest; I want to be with them; I want to learn; someday, will I grow? Will my fears dispel? Will I have my own wife? In the next decade, who will I be? Will we keep our gains? Soon to come are uncountable storms; the coolness of the air is invigorating, though—

Bill Miller

OH, TO BE Bill Miller, the unreachable one with the invulnerable eyes, the 35-speed bike, the sixty years more of life and a future as good as real. To be Bill Miller of the nasal tones, riding fast, with a personality built to anger, to steam; to own an absence of self-responsibility; to smile, then ride across the green, full of Bill Millerness evanescent through the pores, ears flat and unseen. To possess sharp, yet bland facial bones, to be Bill Miller in that unwavering way: distant, yet with a vast antidotal protection from nerves; the reach of the hand, the achievable speed of the road; to be the only one, not twins or difficulty but only Bill Miller, then again, then more; to be the denying one always; to be clean and correct from birth, lacking corpuscular problems, free of sloughs of worried schisms; to be simply and solidly Bill Miller racing the bike down the road, the neutral one of normalcy, culture, diversity, only himself always and again, the racing, unharrowed one drinking a Coke, demonstrating this condition of being an odorless, Coke-drinking person by drinking further Cokes; to own an enduring, monolith stare; to be a judge—that is, to be without burden, yet lightly engaged. To be both ways; to be unswarmed, inviolate, not unnoticed, but instead freely and sexually Bill Miller insofar as unassailability goes; now in a car, owning the car, driving to all righteous places along the road: to major, not minor brands; driving to private land close to, yet distinct from, public land, while the public land, at the moment glimpsed, suddenly never being public again, and right alongside it, Bill Miller thundering along, thin yet broad, present always, yet never absorbed, grinning just slightly; to be self-designed, streamlined, which is less, meaning more, which is Bill Miller just exactly where he was, riding upon this line down the road, moving to the right, then left, then back again; to escape just for fun, and then to return; no matter for Bill Miller, light as if nothing, strong as the vaunted stone, to be just this tall, advantaged form driving a car down the immaculate road; and explicitly not to be a donkey, not to own a donkey but a car, to race ahead and be already gone before the donkey's snout was hacked off and upon the ground.

Lax Forb

WHEN LEAVES FALL dogmatically to the ground and the wind pulls them in streaks, no one is at fault; as every house and yard stands in full color, the earth is generating its own art. The people in Cincinnati knew this; Lax knew it too. But he did not know how life can change.

Lax Forb was, like all young men, starting a new business, living in style, owning large numbers of ties. He heard a sound in his ears; he came from a family of four or five; the sound was a river that would not end. The night was in the river and in the bedrooms smelling of skin, and the family stayed together because they had to. There were no struggles of any kind. Long ago, though, something had happened to Lax's mother, it had to do with a soldier, no one knew exactly, but the mother let on a bit about it every day, clenching this occurrence like a jewel or weapon in her hand. At night she smiled indolently to the violet TV.

Lax was unaffected by his entire family, as he often remarked, downing a glass of lukewarm buttermilk. Each morning he woke, the sunlight stained his eyes with a yellowness, an illusion that there was such a thing as permanence. Lax would drive to work then, ordering, stocking, re-adding sales, for each month was the busiest, and no one had any reason to think of ruin.

One night though, when sitting down to dinner at the age of twenty-nine, Lax had a spell. For the first time in his life, a sweat of panic broke on his lip. He trembled, eyes darting to the closed cupboards, panting, fearful because his parents' and siblings' faces all looked just like monsters' or fruit bats'. He raced from the table, spilling his plate, diving onto his bed, and finally he slept.

When Lax woke, everything was fine. He read a news magazine that told of a coming war, and he clipped his toenails. The stillness of the bedroom held him the way he liked and he was immune to change.

On Tuesday, a woman entered Lax's place of business. She was named Lady and wore a thick, pink sweater. Lax strode near Lady and then had a feeling of holding back going to the bathroom. Lady was pretty, and a shoe model. For this reason, she must protect her feet at all times, she said, laughing, not explaining if this were a joke, taking Lax's arm, strolling with him around the circumference of the store.

When they were married, they returned like birds again and again to their new home with food, collecting it in deep storage spaces. The pair laughed together, the blur of their relationship all over their minds. As he did not know her well, Lax assumed she was just the same as he; and now the months were filled with awfully strange, new activities, and, for Lax, the togetherness created a nausea and unpleasant awareness of his skin.

Lady was often grumpy. But at night, in her private sleep, meaning stole across her face, and it softened with calm.

Lax could not determine if he liked Lady, though she had begun a practice of petting his head, face, and ears; it was all part of the bargain, as she observed once loudly in the middle of the night. Lax enjoyed the face-petting, and it might occur anywhere; for example, near the mailbox, though no one could really predict.

He breathed lungfuls of snowy plains air. It was Christmas. Lax closed the front door and turned to Lady, not at all comfortable with his life, pretending otherwise. "You look beautiful," he told her, "like flowers, like everything alive—trees, grass, a goat—"

"Shut up," Lady said, staring into the fire.

In the morning, Lax started the car, with Lady riding beside him on the way to work; she petted his face. The car buzzed along the bare road. Lady peered through the windshield. "Look at that, won't you," she said flatly.

Snow and ice were rushing down from the sky; lines of dry snow caked the highway. Sheets of air flailed, expressing the same tumult again and again. Lady dropped her head, falling asleep.

The car slunk up the hill, encased by snow. Lax looked down to his insubstantial pants legs, breathing fast, and he grew alarmed because, abruptly, he could not feel himself exist. He stopped the car, listening to sparks of ice on the roof, and beyond that, to saturations of silence that were too difficult to be lovely.

He jiggled Lady's hand. "I think I'm having a spell!"

"What of it?" Lady said, waking.

His body was evaporating, Lax told her.

"Oh, don't pay any attention to that feeling—it's imaginary!" she said, getting out her mints.

"Pet my head now!" he cried.

"I'm tired of you and of everything you want," Lady said. "I have my career to think of!" She leapt from the car, instantly hailing a taxi, and it shot away on the snow-doused road where Lax could scarcely see.

Lax got mad. Lady had never run away like this before, and no one ever should. He gunned his car and went after the taxi.

The distance was wide, and the cars floated with speed; they streaked past a highway sign, and Lax made out a word: AKRON.

"Dammit!" said Lax. He was going farther than he had planned.

Lax did not know Akron. Perhaps Lady did, and perhaps it was a wonderful place where she would find a new life; yet if that happened, Lax felt he would fly apart in shards, and he wanted only to stand near the mailbox while Lady petted his face and head.

Snow became rain. A flashing sign along the highway warned everyone to pay strict attention to the road, and the sign went on to explain that this enormous storm had something to do with the foulness of the earth, and human greed and immaturity too, and that more information detailing causality would be available soon, but Lax could not bother to stop.

The taxi turned onto a small road. It rolled toward a wooden bridge, stopping. Lax followed, pulling alongside. The adjacent snow field induced a hopefulness in him, the sense of a barrier beyond which everything would be fine.

The driver slipped from the cab. He pointed to the bridge, where thin wood shavings covered the planks. "See those chips?" the driver called to Lax. His breath smoked with cold. "Those chips weaken the bridge. They're poisonous to the bridge."

"That's not true!" Lax called back.

"No, no, my friend. Someone destructive is playing a prank—wants to see this bridge come down. He's probably hiding over there." The driver indicated the river bank. "He thinks he won't be seen in this storm and perhaps he won't. There's danger around here—some people don't know about it. That's why I tell you this now," the driver said. "We can't take this bridge to Akron. Let's take another road."

"I don't want to go to Akron!" said Lax, but the driver slammed the cab door. Lax glimpsed Lady's shadowy profile inside. "Lady!" he called, and the taxi spun away.

Lax was sick. He drove on. Sweat dripped from his lip. He had forgotten his life's routine; he had always been following the taxi, it seemed.

To his amazement, Lady stood on the highway's edge near a rest stop, waving him down.

She opened the door, well-groomed and alert. "Don't talk to me, Lax. Just drive home," she said, her lashes releasing particles of snow.

With tears on his lips, Lax lay his head back and drove, telling Lady of his spells, and the sudden sensations that he did not exist. He murmured half-words then, dozing, chuckling, weakly angling his foot on the gas pedal as Lady used a flat palm to help steer the wheel.

Firmly and softly, Lady then informed Lax that she was Jewish, but that nevertheless, she believed in large personal sacrifice. She understood Lax's spells were difficult, and she would help him by looking something up in the phone book, she said.

"Lax," she summarized. "It's too hard to be alone. I'll stay with you. And I'll pet your face."

He raised his head. "Oh, Lady," he said. "Let's go to Rome."

As their jet lifted up, Lady slept in her seat, and Lax gazed at the golden cryptic city lights below. Dully, he knew that soon he would soon have another spell; soon enough, it was upon him. As he sat there, it seemed the sides of his chest were opening, slipping away, corollaries to the sky.

A pilot strode through the aisle.

"Would you like a book of puzzles?" the pilot smiled, offering the little paper books to passengers. He handed one off to Lax, who agitatedly threw it down.

The pilot looked at him, then gazed at Lady. He nodded approvingly. "Look at that," the pilot whispered to Lax. "That's a nice wife. With her, there's no need to be the tough guy. The soft parts of you can come out. That's how it is between male and female."

"I don't need the soft parts to come out," Lax replied. "I need them to go back in."

"You joker! Ha-ha!" The pilot boxed Lax on the ear.

The plane pitched, and Lax stared at the wrinkled water below. "Will the plane crash?" he asked the pilot nervously.

"Hmm. It could," explained the pilot, "if an engine quits, or an aileron snaps. The air is a hard master, you see. Yet wouldn't it be a beautiful way to die, so high up in the sky? I've imagined it many times, I don't mind telling you. I wonder if God is in the sun?"

Lax drew a breath.

The plane tipped sideways. "Whoa! You were right—this plane is going down," the pilot observed, strolling away.

Lax breathed fast. He cried, knowing that, just as he had feared, he would no longer exist and would soon meld with the blankness of the sky. "My spells weren't imaginary—they were real," he gagged.

The jet was flying too slowly to have the air's support. It dropped and spun, hitting the water, though not too hard. The water buoyed the plane in a way the air had not.

They picked their way out of the wreck, shoeless. "Dammit!" said Lady.

Flood lamps poured across the orange safety raft. Lax's pants were torn. The skin of his calf was loose and babyish, and he tried to cover it with his palm. Water surrounded, with seed-like lights in the distance, at the shore.

"Is it over?" he asked.

"What do you think?" said Lady.

Pat Smash

A MAN IN Cincinnati had two sides, but why? No one knew why.

That man's name was Pat Smash.

Pat was strong. He knew how to turn away. Pat Smash was appropriate. After showering, he glistened and he would be fine. He lived quietly in his own home the way everyone should.

As a youth, Pat played a game that often made him tingle. He held a short male doll before him, wondering who—he or the doll—would be killed first. He waited. From the porch he saw the heavy car which bore his father home. He ran to his room, always the same, the world around him fresh as a bare red embryo before the moment it was gashed.

Pat Smash did not really care for the tension of life.

At West Falls High, Pat was one of the gang, or so he told his mother, though at lunchtime he usually whittled quietly in a corner. Joey Brill came and pushed a white donut into Pat's eye. This bothered Pat. As he fell backward to the floor, he saw how time grows slower. The hallway and the intensity of its geometry shimmered before him.

The next year, a red-haired girl remarked casually, leaning against the locker, that Pat Smash was an up-and-coming man. "Take bees, for example," she said. "If a bee gets hurt, he has no doctor to help. Bees don't have hospitals, because they don't have brains. Nor do they have free will. Pat, you have both," said the red-haired girl, storming away.

Pat grinned: so it was to be. Suddenly Pat Smash dove headlong into a retail career. He quit school and purchased his own home.

One night, Pat slept. The door to his house opened, allowing a humid wind inside. Unbeknownst to Pat, a poor, weak family entered the house. The family was troubled. The four of them had greasy hair and dirty skin, because they were poor. The family crept upon the stairs, waiting.

As Pat Smash woke the next morning, he felt divided about the family of four. He watched them as they huddled on the stairs, weak and nervous. The poor, thin, shirtless father leaned to his poor string-haired children; the mother passively held a cloth. The family seemed hungry. Pat said, "Would you like a pizza?"

The family said yes.

Pat did not give them one. Instead, he left the house, not caring for these folks and their difficult brown shoes. At his desk he worked all day gloomy. "They shouldn't be so poor," he hollered into his hand. "Why are they that way, and why did they come to Cincinnati?"

Grumpiness was strong in Pat Smash as he walked. "They need social services. I will help them get it," he vowed. But upon returning home, Pat loosened his tie and did nothing. The mother lay against the daughter, who drooled in sleep; another child had dry, hot eyes. "Why are you so damned lifeless?" he demanded, and for the first time Pat Smash went out of control. He overturned some papers. He ran to the kitchen, then back. Pat felt he had nowhere to stand. He sped downstairs to his workbench and furiously designed a motor boat. The galley would hold forty. He dug his heels into the carpet, for he could not bear this family or its habits. Pat Smash ran upstairs and threw some orange peels near the family's feet. He felt their soft eyes latch to him. The father threaded thin, ascetic fingers through his long beard. Pat became wild with discomfort. He hid.

Under the bed upstairs, Pat Smash got mad. "He's the one who should be ashamed!" he said. "They're the ones who are such a dirty, poor mess!"

Pat surged from his bedroom and relocated into the living room, so he would never have to use the stairs or see the poor family again.

In two weeks, Pat approached the stairs. There he saw a slope of filthy, silty soot upon the carpeting, piling around the family's knees and legs.

"They are getting poorer," Pat said.

The family was in the soot, all on hands and knees, bellies down, and upon hearing Pat Smash's voice, each lifted a sooty face to him, the silhouette of each face, Pat now saw, identical. The entire family looked alike. They looked like Pat.

Now something raced in Pat Smash. It spread through him and a trembling vibrated in his ears. A bolt fled through his stomach, a loose wire in the groin, something coming to get him, running too slowly to be believed. It was a wild hog. The hog was not stable. It bucked. Pat Smash sweated, turning round and round, crashing into the banister, fearing the family would never leave. Yet he could not imagine life without them. So Pat sobbed, dropping to his knees in the soot, lost between his two sides.

He ran to the kitchen, took up an iron, and returned. He hit the family, because it was too much trouble. Pat killed the family. They lay still and their wet flesh shone. "Yah!" said Pat, then went to the bathroom for forty-five minutes.

He sped from the house in his car. Pat Smash was all right.

Believing It Was George Harrison

In Sebucán, a suburb north of Caracas, people try madly at all times to appear happy and carefree. But two Septembers ago, the Estrella Roja had won an afternoon game, and parts of the city were authentically celebrating. I slid out of a taxi after work, walking toward the embassy party. Cars of hooting, hollering people rocked past and that was easy enough to enjoy.

There was no guard at the condo's encircling wire fence. A group of locals, all women, were heading into the condo complex, too, laughing so loudly that I veered to the side, waiting for them to pass. Filing through the revolving door, they turned to stare back at me. North Americans, so full of Calvinist grimness, are easy to spot.

That night I had not wanted to contend with anything much. Finished with the staff training, I was tired. The lobby walls were sweating, as if struggling, but on the fifth floor, Heather's condo was airy, with its bamboo floors and furniture of spare design.

A long table was set with sand-and-green Denby platters. This is no potluck, I thought; clearly that had been a joke. There were salvers of breads and sauciers of peppery oils in reds and greens; Heather charged between the kitchen's swinging door and the main room, setting down pitchers of pink batido crowded with fingerlike ice cubes, and the second maid followed, watching. Through the balcony's row of sheer curtains, I glimpsed the mountains' sage and dusty skin.

In a far corner of the adjoining room, a wire, cagelike partition sat on the floor, enclosing some green hay or alfalfa. Inside was a small white rabbit, ruminating, hunched. Well, all parties need a bunny, I thought, as I looked for a place to put my bag. Maybe to consume the leftover vegetables? Down the hallway, the first door was closed. When Heather appeared, I gestured.

"…?"

"Oh, Helmut's in there," she said brusquely, passing. Her skirt was the kind of cotton so clean and white it appears blue. Helmut was a new boyfriend or another pet, I guessed. Through her diplomat ex-husband, Heather had gotten her embassy job, though she never spoke the ex's name. She had considered leaving this country after her brother back home had grown very sick, but she just couldn't do it. So she would live here always.

I stood outside the door, not enjoying the idea of a roomful of people. I was too new to have good friends here. The TV, muffled behind the door, said: "Some things in life are real, some are not!" I leaned into another room down the hall, elaborate with carved baseboards, and dropped my bag inside.

In the hallway I stood quiet as a knob, amazed that people in the next room had things to discuss. What could they be telling each other?

Now Heather was talking to Sara, one of the visa secretaries, about a garlic recipe, and kept saying "the vegetable."

"You bake the vegetable at a lower heat than usual. And you pour on some chicken broth and baste the vegetable every so often." This noun, combined with the day's heat and the fact that everyone already knows this recipe, made me furious. Soon Heather introduced me to Julia, a painter, whose crocheted dress was pink and gray, the colors of an old cat. But the dress was lovely and its knitted loops a little mesmerizing;

they formed a spreading chain that could not end.

Beside me at the table stood a celebrity, Daisy Fuentes. Tall as a soldier, curvy and gorgeous, she chatted, conscious of her own presence. She seemed pleasant, though I could tell she would set limits swiftly if she wanted to. This social circle was accustomed to the occasional presence of famous people, though I was not; awkwardly, I drifted again toward Heather, who was routing some mayonnaise into a ramekin. Heather never allowed her maids to do anything, so they stood by like everyone else, taking in Fuentes's glamour.

Whispering, I asked, "Why is *she* here?" Heather looked up through her brown bangs. Around the table, a few people leaned in for the morsel of her reply: "She's in town for some benefit and came with Maria."

This meant Maria Vegas, the country's minister of nutrition, who stood a few feet away, eating toast. Soon, Fuentes was talking to the embassy's deputy chief, looking significantly bored. Her feet were enormous. The deep-pocketed white blouse she wore was a designer's arch commentary about an apron. The small stir over Fuentes died down as people refilled their glasses and plates; when the deputy chief left, Fuentes suddenly seemed at a loss and alone.

"Are you settling in?" Julia asked me kindly. Heather, still annoyed by something to do with the mayonnaise, stalked back to the kitchen.

Then music descended, the kind of fast club track filled with heart-skipping beats and haunting minor strains. Some TV soap-opera actors arrived. This party was really an outlier, I decided, atypically casual, though still restrained in the embassy way. More food onto the tables. The head maid reached into a cabinet, extracting what looked like a butter curler, and then dived back into the kitchen. The second maid stood deep in thought.

Someone said sarcastically, laughing, "Oh, and I'm the Duke of Knightsbridge!" This was Richie, a decorator friend of Heather's who recently had shed his entire given name, Michael Ricardo Tankersly

Custorquia, after a dispute with his disapproving family. Richie also had taken a separate Zen name, which I could never remember, that he used during meditation practice.

"Things okay?" I asked him.

"Everything's heaven," he said, smoking. His partner, a wickedly funny man from Finland, stood on the far side of the room.

"What did your family say about the name change?"

"Nothing. I don't hear from them." He smiled, but his eyes were marbled with emotion.

"I'm sorry."

"Don't be—I just want to go on, live, have fun. My family is just not sensitive to suffering."

"Not everyone is," I said.

"Which is strange—because suffering's everywhere." he said. Inside a napkin, he carried some sauce-covered bread. "If you intend to take a dime out of your pocket," he said, "and you accidentally take a nickel out instead, even that is suffering. A Zen master told me so."

"How the hell is that suffering?" I said.

He seemed disappointed that I didn't understand. "The world will never be the perfect place we want it to be."

"Richie!" It was Sara, walking up to us. She hugged him and told him he looked great.

Then Julia returned and pointed out a man and woman in the next room, near-cuddling in a window-seat. The sight of them made me feel lifeless. "Who is *she*?" Sara murmured.

"I have no idea," said Julia.

"I've seen him," Richie said. "He's on the first floor."

"No, he works in the Fulbright office," I said.

"What-have-you," Sara waved it away. "Look how meaty and big he is!"

"He *is* pretty hefty, actually," I said.

"And she's a little skewer, not ninety pounds," said Julia.

"Doesn't matter," said Sara. "The main thing is that he can get it in."

We laughed like children. "Oh, God, Sara!" It was Renata, another co-worker, her face in her hands with laughter, wiping red eyes. From across the table, Heather glared, as if suspecting our joke was at someone's expense. She set down platters of a multicolored terrine and a roast with sauce so deep brown that it was nearly purple.

Across the room, on the far side of the archway, I saw George Harrison pouring water into a glass from a carafe. Floating orange slices and ice slid in the stream, yet the bubbling water moved slowly enough to look like a gel. The sad dance music beat through the rooms. Harrison glanced around a moment, neutral faced, and then greeted another guest, a Caraqueño, certainly, and most likely a pensioner. Harrison mock admonished the man with something like, "Hey, old timer!" and the two embraced and settled into a conversation.

Other guests noticed Harrison, too, exchanging looks, but no one said a word.

I glanced between Fuentes, who was now in another conversation, and Harrison: both celebrities had dark, large facial moles I never had noticed before. Well, I thought: who on earth has no wens? The moles bothered me, though, and I checked them repeatedly, perhaps hoping they would vanish. The music pounded. The previous moment's enjoyment with Sara, Richie, and Julia had evaporated, and I didn't know where they had gone. Coming to this country had been a mistake for me, of course. But there was nothing I could do about it now. With my tiredness, I wanted to return to the residence hotel, yet Harrison, or whoever looked like him, made me want to stay.

"Did you see those moles?" I asked Heather. She looked at me for moment, then swallowed icy wine.

A group of college students from Simón Bolívar arrived, among them,

I heard someone say, the daughter of an American professor. She was shockingly pretty and energetic, with a dark, hanging wall of hair. She danced a bit next to her friends as they found drinks, and from her full, calm face, I decided that never once had she been seriously abandoned. In a few moments, the students noticed Harrison, and their group began to buzz.

The girl's skirt was intensely blue. She ventured to the archway, studying Harrison, then went back to her friends, gesturing behind her, mouthing words that looked like "What the hell?" Scanning the room, she tried to find eyes to reflect her astonishment, but the guests were aloof.

She drank water, then thumped her glass on the table. Then she got louder. "Whoa, do you see?" she said, looking around. "WHOA!" A few people looked disturbed by this. In the other room, Harrison was still hearing out the older man, looking at the floor, nodding at it.

Everyone was staring at him now, of course, not just the girl. His hair was brushy and short, brown and salt. The inky eyes, fine nose, and ascetic upper lip all were as familiar as if parts of our mothers' faces. It looked *just like* him, massive eyebrows included.

"Did you invite him, Heather?" Renata laughed, tipsy.

"Obviously not."

The dance music sparked onward, covering all of us in rhythm.

"I mean. *George Harrison?* How is that possible?" The girl couldn't seem to tolerate it. She turned like a revolving toy, rudely cutting in front of the mayor's assistant, who, gripping a phone and several pens in the same hand, looked as worried as ever. With her bronzed, sandaled feet, the girl then moved toward a man in a pale suit, gripping his arm, talking at him. This was Victor Leizaola, a patrician government lawyer; I'd seen him at another party. He looked down to the girl's accosting hand, freezing her away: "Excuse me, young lady."

It didn't deter her. Wiping her damp face, treading around the table, she pointed at Harrison through a raised palm, and, in general, expressed so much astonishment that no one else had to.

"I know, right, a little weird," a woman said finally at the far end of the table, raising a cough-syrup-pink fingernail to an eyebrow, scratching. "I mean, you think you've seen everything, and then." She shrugged.

"What's wrong with you people?" the girl said above the music to those of us nearby. "Why isn't anyone saying anything?"

Sara faced her. "I think, first of all, you'd better mind your manners," she said. "There are a thousand explanations, so don't get carried away."

"A thousand?" the girl said, mouth pulled tight. "No, there are no thousand—there can only be one!"

Richie whispered, "She doesn't seem stable."

"How could she be? She's a student, and probably not a very good one," said Asko, his boyfriend.

"Look, dear, if you're that upset, go the hell over and *talk* to him. Get to the bottom of things." This was a book writer, a Londoner; I had met him once before.

But no one, including the girl, was so inclined. Harrison, or whoever looked like him, was too unnerving. It had something to do with the large darkness of his eyes, or perhaps his startlingly filthy jacket.

"Is this a joke?" the girl now flared at Lazlo Miranda, a magazine editor. "Are you not concerned? Could there be something *mystical* going on?" A quiver ran at the bottom of her voice. Everyone stood around, watching her perform.

Then Heather stood before her. "Honey. Listen. What's your name?"

"Saundra."

"Okay, Saundra—"

"Don't patronize me," Saundra said. "The man is *dead*. How can he be here?"

"Saundra, this is my house," said Heather, "and you are out of order. You will calm yourself down, or you will leave."

Under this command, Saundra retreated to her friends. On the high-backed chairs, the students commiserated. "Maybe we're *all* dead," I heard one of them say.

Moving slowly past the table and toward them, Lazlo paused with his drink, saying to her, "Just think for a moment. It's a lookalike, simply. That's it."

Then the electricity cut out. The condo blinked into darkness and the music drained away. "Ooh!" rose through the room, along with cries of irritation from neighboring condo units. Immediately, Heather, the maids, and, for some reason, Leizaola, began rooting in drawers for candles, lighting them. We installed these in various candelabras that the maids hauled out.

"I didn't hear anything about rationing for tonight," said Sara.

"It could be a real outage," another voice said.

From the other room came the crashing, ringing sound of wire, and I knew that someone had knocked over the rabbit's enclosure.

"Uh-oh," said Asko.

Once the candlelight was established, the party simply rolled on in a different color. Immediately, the guests checked for Harrison; now he was in the next room with the pensioner, leaning on the back wall near the window seat, looking at the older man with a scant smile. Someone opened the balcony windows fully, and a strong, warm breeze tore through. Guests relit the candles, returned to the table, replenished their plates.

"Seriously," Asko said, his face and lips tawny with candlelight. "Say that *is* George Harrison. That he's somehow with us again. The question is, what will he do? Will he get a job? I mean—not for the money. But he's got to do something with himself."

"The thought of it!" said Sara. "To come back, and then to go looking for a job!"

Julia said: "Well, you'd probably want to pursue things you'd never had a chance to. You'd go for your passion, right? I'd go for filmmaking, if it were me."

"He could open a restaurant," said Renata.

"He'd have to go in with a few partners," said the book writer. "And that's the only way to do it—for anyone, not just businesspeople or the dead."

"They could start a series of restaurants," said Asko. "Steak and pork."

"To hell with that!" said Leizaola, stepping into the group. "I'd go sailing."

"But, I mean," Julia said softly, "this happens, doesn't it? The dead sometimes find a way back. Christ, it happens."

"Oh! That we are witnessing it!" Leizaola's wife said, moving close to her husband, hand on her neck.

"I think the general laws, you know, of the universe can—I don't know, bend, sometimes," said Renata. "Why else do we hear so many tales of ghosts and spirits?"

"The dead come back to repair things," said a very petite woman, nearly hidden behind the bread tray.

"Didn't I say go the hell and ask him?" the book writer repeated.

"This is ridiculous," Richie exhorted. "Don't you see? It was a hoax. He didn't die in the first place."

"Oh, my God!" Saundra cried, hearing this, lowering herself back to her chair, mouth open, looking ill. One of her friends held her around the shoulders. Leizaola's wife exhaled, likewise appearing faint.

"His death was a conspiracy, you're saying? Oh, unbelievable," Leizaola grimly addressed Richie, though he was staring at the wall. "It's always the same with you Opposition people—seeing evil plans everywhere."

"It's not like that!" Richie said angrily. "You don't understand the simplest thing—even now, you loyal types don't. And why not? The charade is over, by the way," he said, pausing. "The question is, how can the whole country not die of shame?"

"Richie, *please*," said Sara. "Not now."

Leizaola smiled, unworried. "Ah, nothing," he said. "Drama and tantrums mean nothing."

I noticed that Heather was in the other room, talking to Harrison and the pensioner. The three were laughing, and next to them, Fuentes and another man were laughing too. The whole group seemed to be in on some witticism. I struggled toward them in the half dark, bumping things, but Heather already had left them. Reaching her, I whispered, "My God, Heather, you're so at ease with celebrities!"

"Especially the ones who have cancer."

"Heather!" Nerves jolted my stomach, and I spoke the first thing in my head. "Daisy Fuentes does not have cancer!"

To my right, Fuentes turned, annoyed.

"Okay," Heather said quietly, "she doesn't *have* cancer, but she's *sensitive* to the disease. She's donated to the cause."

I followed her into the kitchen through the swinging door. "And that man—he's some kind of impersonator?"

"Oh, no, it's him," Heather said with a big smile. "That's George Harrison."

"Are you nuts? Please, Heather."

Her upper lip was in shadow. She looked at the backs of her hands. "I..."

"What was the old man talking about with him?"

"Oh, all the delays in the new metro station construction."

"Oh, my God." The rows of knives clinging to the magnetic wall strips seemed too tidy to be real. "How do they know each other?"

"Some nights are just beautiful," Heather said, ignoring me, inhaling the warm kitchen air, closing her eyes in the cesious glow of the stove's nightlight.

"How can he be here?" I said, not meaning to repeat Saundra's words.

Heather reached into the dark refrigerator for another pitcher of batido. "He doesn't know, but he's thirsty."

"Holy goddamn!"

"Don't cuss, dear," she told me. "It's unattractive. Help me bring these trays back in."

"Okay, this is just *your* opinion, after all. Are we drunk?" I said.

"No," she said. "And ... we don't really have to say, I mean define, what's going on here tonight."

This did not sound like Heather at all.

"Are you going to tell everyone?"

"In a minute," she smiled. "But look, why don't you come talk to him yourself? Something you'll remember. After you go back home. For the rest of your life." She picked up the tray.

"I'm afraid," I said.

We pushed through the door.

It wouldn't have been impossible to believe it was him, especially if a person had been through some duress. But all experience, good or bad, dents and compromises us. So it was certain that everyone would believe it was him. Of course I wanted badly to believe him real, too. I had left my home and flown so far away in order to jettison grief, but the grief only had become compressed, a dense parcel that had traveled here with me.

As I guided myself past the table, little jolts twined around my hands and throat.

Everyone was around him in the dark. Under the jacket, his white shirt seemed a big grin.

Saundra was holding the rabbit. "For you," she told him, giggling, and offered it toward him; the rabbit slid to the floor. It loped forward and thumped its foot. The rabbit sat among the group, white ears rotating. Its odor was warm, lovely, and ancient.

"Thank you," his voice buzzed, and Saundra was smitten.

True, he had once existed, then stopped, but somehow, that meant that he now could continue to exist. This paradox was like the cool wall of a cave for exploring. You couldn't scale it; you just kept touching it with your hands.

Bluntly, someone asked him: "What is it like?"

He didn't mind. He was holding a cup in his hand. "Fairly nonactive," he said.

"What about music?" It was Sara. Her hair had become flat and lank.

"Ohh, music," he said. The words were bare stations, nodes, on the filament of his voice.

The whole party pressed in.

"Have you found what you've wanted?" asked Fuentes.

Richie sat quietly, tears running over his lips.

"Folks, folks," said Harrison, warmly.

Sitting on the floor, I took in his plainspoken eyes, which contained burdens. Our faces all were lovely in the dim light. His teeth were silver slivers in the dark where the rest of us were breathing. Saundra was leaning on me. "We missed you," she told him.

The Cat

SHE DRANK THE water spasmodically, as if drinking poison, then went to the window. The muscles of her eyes unaffected by the drink after all. Then, with a hardness in her chest, the hardness of a smooth, creamy-layered shell, she lay down, this surface undisturbed by the twitching of her nervous fingers at her sides.

Every day was the same: to lie on the plankish bed after class, to fall asleep with propulsive force. At six-thirty in the evening she would wake, mouth dry, full of a sense of rawness—herself—with the ivory shell momentarily gone, and in its place lay the inadequate barrier of her skin, so permeable or disappointing.

The woman did not like easy pleasures like food or television. There was always more work to do—completing more classes for one thing, so she could finish school and support the two of them better, rent a nicer apartment.

Reaching with her fingers, she touched her damp temple where the hair was darker, denser, more orderly. She went to the window. The air was warmer today, and she could not relax.

Easily half a lifetime is wasted in sleeping and driving, a teacher in high school had once said.

With her skinny legs and resemblance to her parents, she felt as fragile as she had when a girl. She was fifty-three and required herself to lie still on the bed every day after her last class, before she fed her mother, but today it was spring and the idea of the brief nap disturbed her. Because she must work harder, stay busier.

The entire body expresses the mind; she had read that once in a book.

The woman turned her head on the thin pillow, driving away her thoughts, not knowing how to lie still any more than does a fly. It was past five forty-five. Scenting the leaves and green in the air, she rose and slid open her room's glass door with the slow, decisive movement of any animal who has no choice but to comply with spring.

The smelly miniature tree growing in a pot on her neighbor's balcony had wrinkled fruits on the branches somewhat like apples, but they were not. From another tree on the small balcony below hers, strong blossoms stood up high, portentous, sweet, and she felt crushed by the life of the odor. I have to start our dinner, Laura thought, but stayed motionless, breathing.

It was nearly nighttime. Across the street on a balcony opposite: a cat. Laura tried to make out the cat's appearance, but she was unable because the city's sunset splayed saturations of gold and orange across the buildings, and the cat had inherited this color.

Her mother yelled her name from the kitchen, and this was not unusual, even if the mother wanted really nothing. In her illness she generally desired to be alone. The mother recently had taken up a habit of obvious pleasure, pushing and pulling her whole hand inside a large open jar of dry rice.

It was not six o'clock, not five-fifty. Even in this apartment, corners behind the refrigerator crackled with unimaginably robust insects, Laura knew; and outside, there were countless creatures, like mice, who needed so much if they intended to really live. Laura's mind began to race with an agitation or anxiety, the residue in her blood from ancestors who had been hunted by enemies.

She switched on a small television, glancing again at the cat on the balcony across the way, then switched it off again.

Laura squeezed her fingers one at a time and considered that her tasks were done so far this week, her routine was on schedule, and the routing of her monthly income was clear. This tidiness consoled and made her look forward to the next year, which would move along in a similarly clear and organized way until she received her final school credits. Then she would get a new job, and she and her mother would move. A breath of self-approval escaped her mouth, and with the shell-like hardness intact in her chest, she had the immunity she desired. Even the hyacinth petals on her balcony glowed with pliancy, yellow-orange in the immodest sunlight, and they were inviolable because their leaves would always grow in the same shape. Laura sat down.

Through the open door she watched the cat washing itself, deeply inside its equilibrium. It was preparing to sleep. Its ear rotated to receive a sound, the voice of a neighbor girl on the balcony next to Laura's. The girl was about ten and wore a looping bead necklace. Beads were wrapped around her long hair. She was at the railing, humming, then mouthing words as if from a song.

In the kitchen Laura's mother vocalized again, wanting water, or a blanket, or nothing. Then there came the sound of ice rattling onto the floor.

Laura stepped onto the balcony and looked down to cars sliding horizontally across the transom of the city; on the hill they rolled faster, pleasingly, falling with gravity because there was no other choice. The sun blew behind cloud cover and dusk arrived, a relief, a gift from the machinery of space.

The cat washed its tail. Now she could see: it really was an orange cat.

She stared at the cat and had an impulse in her mind to call her grown daughter who lived in the East, but not now. She tasted the sharp, sooty air, glancing at the cat's cream belly, bending forward so the buttons on her jumper strained, smiling at the child next door, the girl with the pink and orange beads around her neck who seemed closer to her now that the sun had gone down.

"Don't you have a cat too?" Laura asked abruptly. She smiled because the child's little face was inviting. She recalled seeing the girl swiping a piece of straw or string at a tiny black-white cat on her terrace, maybe not too recently, and maybe it had been last spring, and maybe it had not even been this particular little girl, but she recalled a child about this age leaning over a cat.

"Don't you?" she asked the girl.

The child spat thickly across the space between the balconies. "Be quiet, bitch," she said, and walked away. Someone else in the girl's apartment—a brother or cousin—stood at the glass door, talking, glancing, laughing, then withdrew.

Laura went back into her room. Standing near the closet, the sounds of the traffic touching her. Nothing has changed, she told herself lightly.

The clock did not say 6:11 or 6:17; breathing, she waited for the clock to resume and she looked at the cat, whose comfort in dozing caused her to feel enraged.

Now the girl on the balcony sat in a chair, her back to Laura, and appeared from behind to be whittling or peeling something, given the short, sharp movements of her shoulders, but Laura knew this was probably not so. Uncertainty covered her like a stole. Being uncertain is like being blind, Laura sensed, and her heart raced.

Don't think about anything, she told herself, and thudded her upper arm with her fist. She watched the cat, that observant orange cloud with yellow eyes which had watched the exchange with the neighbor girl. The eyes' lenses curving like water. The adhesive patch of the cat's nose.

Laura drifted back out to the balcony again, unable to help glancing at the girl. It was a flaw to be weak and pleading, she knew, but could not stop herself from leaning over the railing. "You know I've lived here for a long time, right?" she called to the girl. "Can I ask you something?"

The girl turned around.

"Well, can I?" said Laura.

The girl did not deliberate. "I said shut up, fat bitch." She went back inside the apartment where she lived.

There, she told herself, and, with nothing to do with her hands, wiped them on her skirt, not recalling the last unkind words from her grown daughter, the daughter who was overly-brusque and set a time limit for phone calls—ten minutes. Instead, Laura heard the sound of the running shower over which the daughter, during her last visit, in a towel, had shouted inaudibly to her, the water falling behind masses of curling vapor, which Laura remembered as if it had been paralytic poison. There, she repeated, because she had gotten her dose, and it felt correct; she stared at the cat without seeing, as if her eyes had vanished.

After a half hour, she came back a little. The cat bothered her with its unwillingness to leave, its preference for solitude, its orange leg, its brain of difference. The cat regarded her infuriatingly, he who possessed nothing but his quick ability to keep distant from others, and his skill for murdering with his wide, hairy predator's face while avoiding being murdered.

People are more than rude, they're animals, horrible these days, they have no idea their behavior has consequences, and we are going to just kill each other someday! Isn't it true? Laura squeezed her fingers again, aware her mother needed dinner, aware of her own sense of dramatics, but the dose still ran through her; it hurt. And it was spring.

The sphincter in the air diaphragm inside the human belly, if you could see it, would be the ugliest part of the body, she thought, to her distress, or else the inside of the long flesh covering the soles of the feet. We are so ugly! And I have never cared much for myself; everyone else knows that. Laura squatted on her bedroom floor.

Who really loves me in this world? Who will be with me?

If she had been stunned by the beginnings of a flood against which she was always carefully tightening herself, she also grew radiant and confused, the skin of her face growing warm and rich in color. In the dim bedroom, her folded legs prickling, Laura felt the unexpected freedom that pain can bring. For a moment she became more than herself, an open, radiant gargoyle with dark eyes, asking the question she knew had been asked many times.

Why am I here, when I never gave my consent to exist? Why did you do that to me?

She looked at the cat. The silence, dropping like silt after the question, was familiar. Laura smelled the city, the people's lives around her, their endless work for money, their tiredness. The cat heaved its leg up and began to wash rapidly. Its vulnerable stomach forced her to look away.

The Man Who Was Always a Father

HE HAD ALWAYS been a father, from birth and even before, at a restaurant, in a car, storming back and forth from the office. Often his friends ran to his desk, patting his back, saying, "Calm down, man!" for he breathed in such a heavy way, punching the air, tearing his vest. But this was because he had always been a father and so never had time to develop.

He ran from his office and into the street, for he had one passion, and that was all, really. "Who will be my son?" he shouted at anyone. "I am the father of myself; I wear loose pants. I want a son badly, since I've never had a thought about myself. Won't you hurry and be my son? Consider this. Be my son rapidly, and it will be perfect. Come along," he gestured, but they only regarded him quietly in the noonday sun; then, suitcases in hand, they moved on.

"Barring that," he said, "I will produce you. To produce someone new is best and I will do it unreservedly. I will produce a new son properly though emergently...hurry please, I want to produce someone now very quickly...isn't this wonderful?" he said, and turned to the pillow.

He wanted a son especially badly, in the way of wanting to be strongest and best; not odd though, really, in a nation with a contagion of such fathers and speeding, defensive battle ships. "Hurry," he said, "the production of a son is imminent—I arrived at this idea and will carry it through quickly. I am to produce a son now, for I want really to be living.

I will do it any way I like; say please; it's going to happen any moment now; look at me as I do this—"

He sank back in his chair, squeezing his face. "I'm going to chew some gum," he said, "and let me see the little thing I just made, and even hold it next to me—"

It was wrapped in cloth on the floor, a twisted, scratched twig, all scarred. He said to the twig, "I am the father of myself, and your father; therefore, it reasons that I am your paternal grandfather. I am your provider, too; in fact, I am really you, so you must come now and work at our office. Hurry up, won't you? Do manage your urges." Then he shouted over his shoulder, "I am happy! So I need some coffee and forty copies of everything I own, and when I return, I will need a copy of my son." Then the father stood and left for the park, tying his son to his waist with a wire.

Strolling along, the father said, "Son, I will now tell you the only story I know, and it is this: you have no ancestors. I was the father of myself, so no one came before me or ever raised me. No one will come after me. And since you are not you, neither, for that matter, is anyone themselves at all; everyone you think you see does not really exist; the world, then, is quite empty of people besides, of course, myself, and a few servants, and that is life as we understand it—"

He looked down at the twig's eyes, which were scratches he had dug in the wood with his nails. "Do you hear me?" he asked, then snapped his son in half, hurling him through the park and beyond the fence. "Wait!" he said, but the son already had begun his life in pieces, nothing in the world around him except cars and gravel and, every night, his grieving father, who searched madly for the broken twig, but never found him.

The Tree

Two MEN MET. Living in the blue-hued city, they caught glances, the way adults do. The men grew to know one other quickly; they hurried along the highway exits. A month passed; they knew each other a little. Sometimes they took walks in the forest as if searching together for something.

Steve Sanders, the lawyer of the pair, was nervous. Cal Masters was a library clerk, or as he put it, a "cluck," and heavier, a potato lover, laconic. During this time, the men drove around at night, feeling an elation, a sense of inversion.

When separated during the day, each man thought of the other anxiously. Then they would meet again, eager, finding a sense of return to a warm sea, as if they were not men anymore, but near-eyeless creatures who nevertheless had experienced the surprise of fate. Their meeting had been inevitable, they often said, and they fully believed this.

Steve and Cal each feared terribly that the other man and this entire harmonious experience, this childhood, would be lost.

They joked with friends that they could read one another's thoughts, and this was actually true, when it came to laundry.

Beneath the men rolled time. They were not close to Jesus or any myths of the era. They liked food and business. Though after a while, Cal came to believe in vegetarianism, and later joined an anti-milk group.

"You are so innocent," remarked Steve in wonder one night against the blue pillow.

It was a busy time.

Steve was not generous. All his life he had been extremely interested in gifts, bowel movements, and flows of money through the economic world. He worried that he did not please others, yet he often got angry with people. Cal did not struggle with such things; in keeping with the soft society around him, he usually thought about comfort, entertainment, and meals.

The men quickly bought a townhouse and triple-wide sofas; they also acquired two dogs—white, small terriers—who began to accompany them on their walks. The first dog, Mary, was whole, solid, and strong, but the second dog, Susan, had been born at the age of only thirty conceptual days. So she had weak legs, limped, and had episodes of falling; the men wondered what went through Susan's mind as she fell, gasping, eyes fluttering.

"But what if she dies?" asked Cal some nights, beginning to worry.

"She's not going to die!" said Steve with irritation.

The dogs did well on their walks, even if Susan limped, and sometimes both dogs really laughed and revealed themselves as such tender, inquisitive beings that, for Steve and Cal, the dogs embodied the finest parts of themselves.

They all ate hundreds, then thousands, of meals together. At night, the men, hugging, worried about losing their feelings for one another, and about their dogs.

"I still think we should take them somewhere—they should have new experiences and grow," Cal whispered in the dark.

One spring after a near-gale, Steve and Cal went into the forest with the dogs. Trees formed an impeccable barrier along the path. The men and dogs walked a few miles, then stood in a glade. Cal ate a peach and cleaned the runnels of the pit repeatedly with his mouth; then he spat.

Noon approached. The air had warmed.

The dogs found a wall, and leapt against it, barking playfully, but Steve and Cal soon saw that the wall was actually a wide tree trunk. The tree was rooted along the side of the path. Multiple sub-trunks grew from its center point. The strongest trunk grew out over a grassy drop-off, then went straight up into the air. The tree's top was bushy. A ravine lay below.

"What could be up there?" said Cal.

Steve posited: "A series of nests?"

Cal reached up to grab a branch, then began to climb.

"No!" Steve said. "Cal, that is not smart. We're not here to climb trees—don't do that." Cal did not listen. He climbed higher, and Steve sat down at the base of the tree, waiting. About an hour later, Steve called again. "Cal, come down!"

Rustling near the top of the tree, Cal replied, "I'll be back soon! I'll bring you a souvenir." He climbed higher and was gone.

In anger, Steve wondered if he should go home. He sat by the tree for hours as the dogs explored, then dozed; he grew disoriented with Cal's departure and the madness of the tree, its excessive height, and its many trunks and branches. Steve's life began to seem uncertain to him. Waiting beneath the tree for so long, he felt altered. To fix this, he reached up, beginning to climb furiously, slipping, scraping his hands, leaving the dogs behind in the forest.

At the top of the tree, he climbed over a ledge and saw a small, bland town. Steve walked along the road, seeing a store that sold provisions; he tried, but was unable to go into the store. He walked further, and saw Cal on the empty road. "What the hell are you doing?" he called out.

Cal said nothing.

The men met in the road. Steve shouted inside a panic, "What's wrong? Why aren't you talking?"

"I don't feel very good," said Cal.

"Cal!" Steve said. "The dogs. We have to go back down. The dogs will get lost."

"Well, they've already been down in the forest for a long time, so it isn't going to make any difference now if they wait longer," Cal said.

"I hate you! You changed!" said Steve, smacking Cal on the mouth.

Cal tried to hit Steve back, but Steve blocked the strike. Then Steve chased Cal, trying to tackle him, to punch him down, but Cal outran him, and the two wound up at a house with a large glass skylight angled in the center of its roof. The skylight glinted with color. Beside the house lay a flat lake.

"This is unreal," said Steve, the most unhappy he had ever been. "We have to get back, find the dogs, go home, and go to sleep tonight so we can wake up for work tomorrow. Right?"

"Why?" Cal said coolly.

They proceeded inside the big house. Steve was distracted upon seeing the nice furniture, but his worries returned quickly, centering around the dogs. "How long have we been away from them?" he wondered. He looked at Cal. Neither man could quite recall his purpose in life, if he had ever known it.

Steve's arms and legs grew shaky and numb. He yanked his hands from his pockets, spilling some coins on the floor. "Gosh, those nickels look so big," said Cal, bending over, picking them up.

The men looked out the window. A storm was blowing in. The lake beside the house began to churn and overflow, its water fluttering and rippling, cascading over the lake shore and toward the house. Steve breathed, "This is crazy. Now there's a flood?"

The water seeped through the front door and into the living room; it rose over their shoes and ankles. Cal told Steve to hang on as the water climbed their legs and torsos, shockingly quickly. As the water pulled at their waists, the men tried to make it to the front door; but in the gelid water, they could scarcely move at all.

Trying to survive moment to moment, treading water, Steve hollered piteously. It seemed possible the men might die.

Cal was steadier. "If we die, at least we'll know we took an interesting trip."

"Shut up!" screamed Steve.

In the flood of rising water, beyond the noise he was making, Steve had a regret: he wished he had learned more about why he had lived, and why everything else lived, too.

The men swirled like dolls in the water, rising toward the ceiling. Then, through the big front window, Steve saw Mary swimming in the flood outside, with the weak, gasping Susan to the rear, panting and paddling. "Oh, my God!" Steve yelled, crying, treading water. "Are they trying to say goodbye to us?"

Cal whistled loudly. The dogs heard him through the window and began to swim toward the men. Opening a tiny top pane in the window, Cal began throwing the nickels, one by one, toward the dogs' mouths.

"If only I can get one in," Cal winced, tossing the coins, missing. With the last nickel, he took aim at Susan's panting mouth and said, "If I can't do this, then it was never meant to be." He squeezed his eyes shut and threw. When he opened his eyes, he saw Susan gulping the coin down; then she grew energetic, seeming to laugh. She swam directly to a rope that was floating in the water, and picked it up in her mouth. The rope was attached to the great lower window's latch. Susan pulled the rope away from the house, and the huge pane opened. All the flood water poured smoothly from the house, the men upon its current.

The water lowered Steve and Cal to the ground. As their feet touched down, they found themselves standing in the forest glade beside the tree, where they had begun. The dogs had vanished.

"What the hell happened?" said Steve.

When they were home, the men were able to rest together.

They took new jobs. The men stayed together.

At night, they reflected, each man in his own thoughts, and they drove around the streets in winter, watching the city and how it changed. They adopted two new dogs.

The men and dogs lived in New York City, but they left one year for New Canaan, later returning to New York, where they remained until the area absorbed them.

The Kidney Problem

First there was the kidney problem, and the marriage was very much part of it. The woman pulled through all of it with her body. Despite the voices of robust others on the bus—tremendously loud college students on their cell phones describing all manner of odorous things like foods, sub-basement parties, arguments streaming from their fathers' mouths—despite this, Ivy could not draw their warm breath or health inside her, and she returned home to the wedding preparations, remaining a sufferer of adult-onset spells.

Most common were her episodes of blackout and lost awareness. She had a measurable spell in clinic, too, and a lone doctor, without the company of his team, told Ivy that she probably already had had countless periods of lost consciousness in her life. The bride-to-be was not certain, but agreed that upon occasion she had had numbness and tingling in all extremities, as well as intermittent numbness around the mouth, possibly without even knowing it. She also had experienced total body numbness and tremor. She told the doctor that she had had meningitis eighteen times in her life. She said in the mornings she had an altered feeling, or a sensation of fogginess, and a feeling of falling forward on all fours, though she never actually had fallen, except once, at a brunch. During the wedding week, there was talk of fitting the bride-to-be with shoe orthoses to improve her gait, and reduce the amount of energy needed to walk. There was a question that the bride might have acquired a syndrome with a long name, though no one among the wedding party could remember this name, despite that it included the girlish word "Marie."

It was no one's fault, the bride told another doctor who passed through the clinic's vestibule, that her physical health was balanced as if upon the breadth of a pin.

With the marriage weekend approaching, the groom-to-be had some problems, too. Upon awakening each morning, he would often have a bruised, sore head and tongue; therefore he felt he was having nocturnal seizures. Often in the daytime, he told the technologist, he had spells in which he felt something coming into his body, followed by jerking, thrashing, and forced vocalizations. He was started on an anti-convulsive medication, and this helped. The groom-to-be said that he currently had a detached retina. His mother had died after multiple aneurisms—it was long ago—and his father also had died, but the groom did not know why. Yet overall, the groom's chief worry these days, he said, was excessive sweating, though he was working on adjusting his medications for that.

A few weeks before the wedding, he told a Croatian doctor that he had had fourteen surgeries for scoliosis as a child, as the doctor looked skeptically at his shoulders. In common with the bride, the groom also told of being unable to feel his body from the neck down, and he also reported some general lost awareness of his body. Then he tried to say—the language barrier helped here in some respect, as it allowed the groom's phrases to open, to be less forcibly precise—that he, the groom, felt the socially convulsive nature of the wedding and all the events that would come after, such as deaths and childbirths, were causing huge problems right now. The entire marriage union was careering toward him with a splattering velocity, along with all the fusion-oriented legal papers, and the groom did not like it, he said. The groom's skin had changed.

But the marrieds-to-be were somewhat young, and they had high color this week, and robust, thick complexions such that no one noticed their eczema or anything else, for the bride's and groom's lips were highly active in these days, always moving and pursing expressively while everyone else laughed too, so that the dozens of lip pairs seemed to dominate and lead this wedding party. Meanwhile, the groom's family of cousins and little aunts, and the bride's fractured family, too, continued to collect in the muddy outer reaches of the city.

Soon a pair of wedding planners—a husband and wife—were on the scene, mingling with the family in restaurants; and because the planners were so busy, time got short.

The bride did not tell anyone about her diminished sensation to pin pricks and light touch, and though she was going to take a few moments on Tuesday to do that, she never did. She and her physicians knew, however, that for two years, she had had left hand wasting due to weakening nerve conduction, and she had episodes of shock-like sensations in both arms accompanied by the sound of rushing in her head. She also had occasional fuzzy vision at night on the right side, though this had occurred since the age when a person must break off from herself and never go back— thirteen. The vision spells lasted several minutes each, and occasionally occurred alongside her longer episodes of nighttime fright.

She told the groom about some of her most recent spells, and he retained this information for a day or so, then forgot, because he was busy struggling with longtime decreased vision in the right eye, and, for the past month, absent vision in the left. He also began to have problems with color vision. He was only glad that he was not a female with fibromyalgia awaiting a liver biopsy, or a sufferer of unpredictable tongue movement.

The groom favored his nocturnal seizures over the daytime ones, which tired him more. Also, for the past eleven months, he had suffered frequent spells of déjà vu, and also jamais vu, accompanied by a rising sensation in the stomach.

In addition, the groom was concerned around this time because his brother had a five-month-old child who was currently getting killed vaccines. The brother also was reported to have disposed of a mouse recently. Upon learning about the mouse, the wedding clan worried lightly, briefly, but soon moved away from that fact en masse. There was so much to eat. Downtown at night, below the hills, it was always possible to find chowders, even immediately after supper.

The bride had been told that she had a lesion in the white matter of her brain. Also, the groom's brother had an absence spell after the mouse incident, though he had no subsequent episodes. If the groom's brother had experienced further episodes during the wedding week, it might have helped him insofar as it would have expressed some tension from his, the brother's, body, but, as it happened, it was the groom whose episodes increased in frequency, and this gave everyone partial satisfaction, because someone in the family had to express something.

The doctor on call was either fully deaf or had decreased hearing on both right and left sides, but he was able to understand the bride perfectly with a combination of a hearing aid, lip-reading, and notes. Ivy made the doctor understand something—an accomplishment—near the hotel's central banister, namely that her original kidney problem, being part of her body, would soon be intrinsic to her marriage, and so to her husband and his girth. And while she always had smiled through life, she let the physician know, rigid-faced, that she feared her little body was horrid, dire-smelling, and worse, and that she was using the marriage to force others to accept her and these biological odors and flaws in a way that made both the marriage and the groom's body fraudulent, just like all the rest of the bride's life's facts, which in turn traced back to the sclerotic kidney, which in turn adhered to her mind.

"But it is not all about you," the doctor said with thin patience. Ivy went on, though, explaining that while the marriage was supposed to work hard to bring everyone relief and even grace, it might not, and that her recent-onset episodes now flashed like bright charms before her eyes and the eyes of the sweat-smelling guests. But what she really wanted, she finished, was a calm, comfortable closeness with someone else, and as the doctor understood this, he nodded.

Scoo Boy

THIS WAS MY SCOO BOY, my glider, my street skater, hair long, dark, four tails; he longed to be a boxer someday, a stunt diver, as some boys do. You should have seen him then, my adorable boy born with hope in every flicker of his eye; he was meant to take the money, too, and likewise I was meant to give it to him.

There's no such thing as purity, because that's exclusionary, but this boy shone with the singular uncanny vibration that gives the color copper its peace and glow.

I imagine myself about to give him the money, saying the words, finally: For you.

This takes place just inside the city, where he stayed.

Once I get the money to him, I'm sure to be gratified, exhausted, relieved; I'll sink to my mat, and be able to think once more, about my boy, of course, no other.

He behaves in strange ways I adore, by a code that nobody knows. My gut churns pathetically at the thought of him remaining where he is, in the rankest of places, a half-submerged harbor, the old city hill crest covered with the ooze of the last century's excesses; I blanch at the thought, pains rise, fasten into constellations in my gut, yet I will be all right if I can just get the money to my boy who desperately needs it.

I would like to be able to get him the money, all at once, straight away;

not in installments, just handing it over, my glance forced upward due to the pressure of luminous winds and the flotilla of birds that would have filled the sky then, and with a crash, disappeared.

I miss him insanely like that, in terrible bursts when night comes in. One evening with the others I sat on the crumbling, dust sodden green, waiting hours for a projected film to fall into focus on a screen and begin, sadness inhabiting my gut once again when a well-dressed announcer finally emerged and said, "David, the King of Music, has been dead now sixteen years to the day," tears straining down my face, for we believe we have grasped the passage of time until something shocks such belief away; I wore a sticky wreath around my neck in those days, after the boy was first taken away, to help express the fondness from my heart, like tears from eyes, so it would not collect or obstruct me or make me blind.

He did nothing wrong, truly, for there is no wrong, only what we already know, and have, and have done; the myths are defunct, you know. The armies got soft, and it was far too late; the building facades had already become maroon rust. Many of us disappeared, too; I was told that my father, before last seen, was running down a cobblestone hill, looking in vain for a transparent button. On a sweltering day, at Soldiers' Field, I believe, a begowned, besotted singer wailed to stragglers sitting unsheltered in the sun about the falling down of the world, and a depression the likes of which we had never seen. I stared at my dry, spotted arms, the song burning itself into me; the boy's sweetness was never hidden, I concede, and unless I find the money somehow, with my brittle cunning, duplicitous charm, needle slivers into blisters of want, he will never leave his restraints. Still, my hopes rise toward the incredible rondure of the blank sky, and, I suppose, to heaven, the place they once decided exists apart and pure and benevolent.

If I can get the money to him, I know the boy will be safe. I know he's waiting, silent each evening; after time this makes him quickly older:

that's no good. Can you imagine where he is, caught up in vaguenesses and steam, some sub-slavering factory-like machine, who can quite know, pulling at straps he doesn't need to pull, one after another in confusion and uncertainty; I have fallen, faltered in my terrible dust-covered room imagining this, his bewilderment and sweet striving to maintain some economy of reason and sense throughout. I called him my heartbeat, I remember his up-close scent—despite the years of twisting, arching heat from the sun beating down and the outrage of dust piled between now and then—an elixir of mercury, the saddest element, full of weight and departure, trails of flint, very thin, and of water, not the water we know now, but as it once was, they say, nearly invisible, yet the most gratifying substance imaginable.

Money will illuminate even the saddest of winters, I say.

If I brought him the money, would it somehow reveal to him my hands, my face?

I have so quietly often wondered what deeds I have done that might have caused him to be taken away, my room's chief instrument being the cracked telephone, and who knows murder so deep as speech, they say. On that dry, empty road of apartments, for years dust enthralled, remote, didn't I whisper furiously through the line in so many ways, to get things and money done my way?

He did nothing wrong; it's inside the city he waits, not locked up, yet not at liberty, either—that's the key, the quandary—so that no one can get to him, quite, nor can he leave. I would show him to you at the moment he steps clear, reeking gorgeousness, natural plenary elegance of spirit; wouldn't the money bring him here, accomplish this? Though money is not real, they say, despite it became so, finally, strengthened by the armies, the canons of power—quite obvious forces steering the way—but wouldn't this money impart exactly what we want, and need? Buying him free, setting his impeccable feet into the sand—I dreamed last night of this possibility, of thousands of chaste, awestricken moments beneath the once-living seas, of torrent and rescue and resultant grace; crows, silent helicopters floating to the city's border with goading intent to procure all of this; I remember the grip of his hand; I was older then; now I am young, flying with money and fiendish power to the boy and the center of things, because, after all, power is what we need. I would torture the guardsmen, wring the necks of all cats, smash conveyor belts, bicycles, the histories of our useless kin and their kin before them, to complete this task—the boy is not yet at liberty, so who is? The notion of crime does not impress me in the least, nor do dreams bound to foolish absolutes, or convictions that the old myths are true. But at the moment of liberty, what will this matter for us? He and I, and all the rest, will have escaped within seconds to the tundra or the former capitol of our nation, now overturned in soft clay ruins and vistas, the place where everyone excitedly lives, close to the ground, having buried the words of the dead ones for good, children having untied themselves in a vast and sumptuous explosion of work, calm words in their minds as they skatingly move on, and long after we are gone, who knows what they will have uncovered from our unmentionable era?

The Flier

THIS WAS THE smallest, tiniest expert pilot and resolute flier, rocking back and forth, moving admirably through childhood in just five short days; he returned to his desk, looking everywhere for his boss, but when he asked, "where is my boss?" the entire staff laughed, for he was so out-of-date.

At night circling the mountain top in his plane, and during the day at his office, quiet as a chair, he badly wanted someone to come and be the boss of him; when he found to his shock that there was no immediate, direct, supervisory boss, but only a distant authority in Connecticut, he careened into the reception area, crying, and though it seems strange, this sometimes happens. The little nighttime aviator then fell to the floor in a fit, imploring a lower supervisor to come right now and inhibit him. Disturbed, some colleagues gathered around and built a plastic companion for him, fitted to his contours, for no one wanted to be that close to him.

The man was merely a small pilot with a moustache who had always been friends with anyone, and he could be two ways at once, or any way anyone needed him to be, really, though he was so slow and tired in a way that was hard to understand; perhaps it was a slight depression; he went to sleep at work and woke instantly, describing his plane to anyone who asked. The plane could fly automatically, as the pilot always said, and after landing, he would sigh in his seat; he wanly enjoyed taxiing through the streets, looking out the window to the empty beach.

The rear of his plane was cozy, homey, and moist, with a couch inside, so really, this plane was just like a house. And deep down in the couch lay an exquisite soft spot he should have found by now, but he had not; he tried to reach it each night with his foot as he fell asleep. The plane never crashed, nor bumped, either, nor did anyone hear the motor, as if this all took place outside the atmosphere.

Each day and night of his life this little pilot was always hungry, so he often needed treats; afterward, he would return to the plane; climbing in, he would strap down his ankles and hands. He would thrash back and forth with inconsolable gestures that no one could understand, while his mother, looking on from a distance, shook her head.

She had been away for so long and had become quiet because of the hospital, she said, and a very adult experience there. In the meantime, the little pilot charmed the nurses, then flew off in his plane with its hot, burning scent, glancing for the statue-like mother, who stood in the window, always drab, fussing suddenly with Kleenex. Every time she went away from home, the flier would leave his office and go directly to his plane, where he would buck and shake furiously, in practice, as he always said, for everything.

For twenty-four months he had done this, aching, his scalp sweating, cursing with a kind of trouble and pain he never questioned, really, nor did anyone else; looking out the window, he began to grow afraid; if the coats were not on the coat rack he would know everyone had gone away; he ran to the couch, groping his foot toward the soft spot as he tried to doze, and later he woke to the radio.

The pilot naturally was regularly panicky and sick a bit, for he hated to swim, but water was everywhere, so he had to get a nose clip. Shaking fearfully, he was brave enough to plunge in, just in preparation for being an older swimmer, afterwards enduring a doctor's consultation for his damp groin and bowel and his mother's important thoughts about that and all other areas.

The pilot rammed his plane into the doctor's suite and lawn, with broken glass spread everywhere; then he saw, in a corner of the rubble, the doctor crying, because the doctor had wanted so badly for his patients to love him, but none ever had. The doctor held his face in his hands, since his office was in shards, with the scattering of the glass and nurses' wigs on the ground; but the little flier was already gone, waving, flying above the suburban yards, searching happily and routinely for his mother, scarcely remembering the day before, when she had lain down weeping, then gone inside the silverware drawer, weakly handing him a spoon, then crawling in amongst the forks, and there she would stay with a few wheat crumbs and the dry smell of the drawer. The years pass slowly. The mother lay like a cushion in the dark for so long, ignoring all aspects of sunlight and the circular movements of clouds, and the fact that they all had gotten so much older; nothing was familiar; and beginning at this time, the little flier's eyes became poisoned, though this may have happened earlier. He felt so dark and heavy in his body and stomach while rotely circling the city and mountain.

Surely the mother had forgotten this aviator, flier, office worker, or whoever he was, the one flying low each afternoon above the lawns, though he was extremely busy right now, as it happened, recruiting passengers for Duluth and his many other flight runs.

Then returning one evening from work, opening the door, who should he see but his mother, no longer in the drawer, but all dressed up, smoking angrily in green slacks, leaning against the balcony with its enclosing wall of glass; she walked to the pilot, stuffed some crackers in his mouth, then walked away again.

He flew away, furious, guiding his plane across a great distance to La Jolla, where he collected mud, then bombed it all over the town and its fountain; on top of that, he threw a paper cup; then the flier sped back home, a ridged cake of mud on his airplane's nose. He smiled, ready to show this cake to his mother while sensing at once it was a mistake, which it was, because, as she often had told him, disappearing into the den for hours, she had problems.

He sweated and pounded his hands for the disgrace of this; and the pilot went back to his plane, strapping himself in, forgetting his colleagues and passengers expressly, beginning to buck and twist with the greatest force imaginable, thrashing himself into unconsciousness and the far future where he now lived, this quiet, manipulating pilot, still angry at the valedictorian of his class, holding a strong office job for more than fifteen years, yet always staying at arms' length, preferring to climb into his plane and silently sit.

The pilot never got what he wished, despite opening a savings account; the wheels sprayed gravel as he lifted off, bumping above the coast, nose up, diving, hooting to the clouds, nerves tautening, releasing, suffused with every thinkable feeling because he never really had belonged to her, he knew, and he distinctly heard the air screeching like all the lost children without water, begging.

The World of Barry

BARRY WAS EVERYWHERE, and so easy to marry, full of springtime which is always hope and trust.

The mountains face our living room window, their unsolicitous peaks white and blue; the neighborhood is silent because it was made that way. Barry sits in his armchair, reviewing cases; I steal to him, tilt the brown drink in his mug, pinch the little string overhanging his pocket and tug, pulling more, then more, coiling the cord upon the floor; so much came out of Barry, it is hard to say—

Barry was always familiar, his thick, low, syrupy voice of Boston and mud. Junior partners often exhibit great propulsion and charm; he barrels through the turreted streets downtown, smiling, punning, grabbing a drink, stopping to observe holidays, to pray. Our home is a flexible hinge between the grass ridge and the sky full of dark matter, those invisible forces that hibernate—

Barry often prefers the creamed chicken; our living room table is ruby granite and slate. He bought an oak mule chest and end tables layered with mosaic; at night in the bed I grow down, down, into the cement basement floor of my parents' home while Barry waits, still as a moth—

Like many people, I am an expert in following the rules of my own design, biting back the urge to question these or analyze. Today I tear past Barry's office desk and to the elevators in a rage; why can't he do better, stop laughing, read something beside torts, open his mind, pick up a raisin cake? I dash to the street where by chance my mother and father are driving past, waving gladly with their four hands, throwing popcorn, wearing argyle sweater vests, happy in general about life as it is lived—

Such episodes cause me to feel strange every day.

Barry's vehicle is as large as a small house, with lush, curving metal flanks of midnight green, exhaust pipe thick as a fireman's hose, its mouth pouring white volumes of fog and upon this mouth I must briefly affix my own mouth, in order to best appreciate life, I think, though Barry has never instructed me to do this, nor have TV broadcasts either; yet it is truer than god or the atmosphere—

Barry orders the roasted chicken; we have little to discuss; the newspaper describes a man fitted for a prosthetic face and arms—

Barry drives us home in silence; odors seem to fly from his body—lemon, vulture, brine, it is hard to say, the mingling of all our family's sweat and the opposite of this odor: sense. And Barry is not a bad man, as the dean of law once said; Barry swims agreeably beside my false self, scanning the face of the sky, its mineral dark; at each day's end we see our back door ajar, and lakes up high that we ignore—

All these complex mental processes to keep Barry out; and Barry is cheerful most often, needing no help from the journal club; soon the neighborhood annexation will begin; on so many evenings the chicken is luscious; afterward in town, the foolish clichés of the cinema help keep us silent, thoughtless, separate, and cold—

Barry was originally a chemist, as everyone has ever known; my father told me about Barry long ago when I was small, for I had never satisfied my parents' bodies nor was satisfied by theirs, and screamed unusually, struggling against dependence and the shame rising through it; Barry rarely wants to punish me, though I found ways to make him do it—

Barry's shape is different when he is with me than when he sits alone and reads; Barry wrestles over the idea that god may be cruel, and he implies I should consider this too. But my shape has grown defended and smooth, and I believe Barry's choice in furniture is poor, too: the chest with laurel leaf motif, the heavy cherrywood bookcases rising like vaults to our roof. Unbeknownst to Barry, I set a bowl of milk each day in the rafters to feed a family of sick mice—

Barry and I are very thirsty these days; dust from the warring earth flies through our throats; perhaps we are waiting for the world to mature, to catch up with us. The back side of god is too strange, too vulnerable to hold all of life, Barry worries aloud as he drives; I laugh, feigning anger in a spirit of play, though the danger of our games is what frightens Barry and me—

Barry is not poor or free. Our window holds the soft, alkaline mountain sky, the ribbony road to the old town; the house ticks in the animal dark; the kitchen knives are turned backward and I keep the chicken warm in a soft white sauce, molding it for Barry. In a lapse of self I lure the mice to the floor, pulling aside the kitchen door with the softness of children or breasts, and there they pour in a stream of fur, bathing in our home's warmth; the mice position themselves at the toilet to drink, and this begins to happen every night—

Barry prays for a way into the jumbled panels and panes of god while shifting lanes in his enormous car, and Barry's doubt gives him pain in the mind, foot, and spinal cord; he cares too much what god thinks, which is especially comic at sporting events. Soon, he will take a new case to court, but tonight, there is Barry, standing in the mirror, nude, post-coital worry the flavor of our room; and Barry will make an appointment soon for the urinalysis; there is the council meeting too, and in general, there is too much to do; I scuff across the tile in the far middle of the night, looking through the skylight to mother and father in their part of the sky—

The pepper crust chicken is pretty as a young bride; the fundraiser begins at 6:45; there is the board meeting and the upcoming census, too; my cotton dress like a swab, the Earth held in place by a concerted tie, the sun that will someday break; at night I hold Barry's wrist in my fingers, feeling his absent-minded largesse, the heat of his vacant legs—

My parents hurry from Portage Bay, hoping not to miss the mountain view. Still buried in the bedspread, I see Barry's face, his thoughts straddling duty, succor, ice. We enjoy meals and sweets with enormous oral greed, and Barry favors dark bread, in fact; he is far too tall and big and often makes me laugh, has a hearty appetite for slaw, large genitals, and a voluminous smile; Barry most frequently enjoys the cream mustard chicken, and all in all, Barry has too much inside, too many preferences—

While I am running, Barry thinks deeply about the case. We live on Sky Island Drive, overlooking the parcels of valley land, and Barry and I must not care about preserving that place. He loads his golf clubs into the cargo area, slamming the tail gate; in the front seat I wear microplastic sunglasses, quiet, for Barry must not know that, at night, our house is alive with mice; Barry's shape makes my shape change, ballooning too far then coming back to me strange, so Barry and I are departing in the dinosaur way and will not outlast the sky and stars. Well, what could you say.

Parthenogenetic Grandmother

SHE DID NOT begin to exist because I needed her. Grandmother first emerged in the clearing near my cabin, between hills of trees. She was warm, lively, and driven. Into the admixture went a cruelty that at times resembled the disinterest of nature. Grandmother was no stereotype, however.

She was hairy. The white strands on her head grew to short, soft peaks, like the meringue fur of a Persian cat. As with cats and everyone, Grandmother's self-knowledge, though adequate, was far from complete.

Her birth was not a product of forethought or design; it simply happened. Life advertises itself so lushly.

She could laugh insanely, like the wolf of the forest. The wolf really did eat the bedridden old woman—it had to, many times over, to assure itself of its identity, carry itself to completion.

Our fear of the woods is hardwired but we bar it such that it rarely emerges, except in enclosures like elevators that rise through the thickets of office buildings, high up.

Grandmother was born in a tree. A nurse log, of course. In the hollow must have lain another grandmother, an important one, who cannot or does not contemplate her own generosity, but like the wolf simply grinds away at what she does.

Grandmother's birth process did not require fertilization. This has been done in labs with mice who are fatherless.

It doesn't always go well during labor—messy as hell. Afterward, Grandmother stood and chimed, "Oh, oh, darling," pointing herself in the direction of my cabin. She was identical to her mother and left her immediately, not looking back.

Under its layers of wall-dust, my cabin stands against the sunset. The forest with its stored horrors lies to the east. When I cut back the clearing that year I saw the trees had been struck by infestations and lightening. White fungus discs lay puttied on the trunks, resembling curved, sleeping homunculi. On the day Grandmother was born I was twenty-one and lay flat on my porch, resting, waiting, my cells laboring to turn off the genetic expressions that might have proven aggressive or lethal to the next generation. I breathed, the product of such expressions plus my entire life's worth of thinking, reasoning, my continual disputes with Brother over my lack of generosity.

In her flannel nightgown she arrived. Grandmother's old hand rested on the mailbox. A little yellow sweater over the nightgown. As soon as I saw her I sat up, instantly embedded in love. She worked her way toward me, sleeves and hair littered with termite-dust and the softly pungent shreds of the cedar log's decaying center.

The old woman smiled for the first time in her life. Her face was that of a lambent alien; the floor of the nightgown dragged. The sweater was unpilly. Slippers clean. Her eyebrows tangled with root hairs. I moved to see if she was real from the side, too. Then the other side. Our relationship had begun.

In the woods beyond the clearing the nurse log remained, fragrantly decomposing, far from death. One end nourished a hemlock seedling, and if the other lay crushed and in crumbles, the smallest particles, with stupendous patience, retained their integrity until dissolving into the famous sweetness of the forest floor.

I dusted off my pants, already imagining the proud note I could write to Brother summarizing how I, as the luckiest or best one of the family, was sole witness to Grandmother's birth event.

She and I sat together on the stairs. She would have looked just as fine wearing a gown-like carapace of dark crystals scraped from the identities of rock and sap. "I'm close to you, darling," she sang. Her voice pulled memories from me, its timbre melding in a caramelly way with the voices of my long-gone parents, for the structure and size of our family's vocal membranes always had been identical. I listened closely to the notes and their decay. Surely, I thought, Grandmother is not fully a member of the family, for, born in the forest, she is above it all.

I could not have been further from wrong.

We drank lemonade from stone cups and I returned her smile. Before the smile unwound I smelled an intruder approaching through the long path of the woods. I wanted to tell Grandmother, but stopped; I could not say it, for I was frightened by the prospect of emotional arousal and believed it would render me out of control.

To reassure me, she used spare, comforting, Lutheran phrases that were stingy, I later realized. I was twenty-one and endured well the surprise of her exposed breast beneath the raised white gown, her sudden omnivorous panting. While she slept, I quietly moved my alder chair to the far end of the porch.

She awoke discussing the dry life of the moon. She told how the distance between two cities can alter when the majority of the buildings are on fire. How it is best to break the law on Fridays. I patted a rhythm with my feet on the warm porch planks, ready to hear more. Then Grandmother got up, walked down to the road, and did not return for three days.

I saw her game. Even the forest mouse, descended of large families, knows in his deep brain's refinement the peril of abandonment. The mouse's nose quivers. The frank pain of the upper lip. The snake is vulnerable at the neck and between the ribs and in early spring requires her sisters' wrapping bodies for the edge of warmth their shivering brings.

Grandmother returned but did not explain herself. At night in my chair, I heard her deep laugh. From beneath my blanket I glimpsed her flat, scuffing slippers, her toe joints bent over the soles, curled. "You'd better get ready for winter," she warned, as if I were an incompetent. Then the rain came and the cabin was no longer fully waterproof.

I missed Brother and dreamed of our horseplay but with Grandmother present, I developed a new lens through which to observe the forest and I trained it on her as my anger grew.

Over the days she had enough time to drop the innocent act, to stop saying "Oh, really? I had no idea," so as to lure me, as well as others—the mailman—but she did not bother. She knew far more than she let on. She could have stopped her scoffing attitude, become less unpredictable, more mature; she could have changed.

"You're only loved as much as you believe you are," she said arrogantly, standing at the top of the stairs.

From the deep grammar of our genes, our family color, snow, on tree-filled hills of rage emerged. Like many people, I did not know the points at which I could apply leverage. I could describe the forest but I could not detail its workings. I knew the forest's clues and signs but I was unlearned as to what these precisely meant.

The game took another edge. She stopped talking to me for periods of time that only she chose. Sharp and manipulative, she needed to depend on me for such interactions and needed me to be dependent, too.

The intruder was still en route. He had been for days, carrying a shovel or radio. I heard his insane breathing in my mind at a distance of miles. Intuition told me he was a stranger, but intuition is blunted by character, even on good days, and so is ever incomplete.

"Now you owe me," Grandmother said unbelievably, as if she had the right, her head burgeoning, turning in the doorway. She hid a pot of coffee so I could not have it, absurdly. The mailman stopped delivering letters because Grandmother told him I hated him and wanted no mail.

It stank. The cabin whirled and events occurred too quickly. Grandmother made it clear she wanted to have some special tie to me based on the small capricious favors that would leave me indebted or obligated to her. She hinted this tie would be illicit in some way and tried to tantalize me with promises of future gentleness and even money while being unreliable. I was twenty-one and had fewer rights than she.

Later the mailman returned, smiling anxiously, bringing a load of letters from the family; these had been piling up in his vehicle, he said. The mailman chatted. His route, he said, was a good one. "My union is strong," he said, while Grandmother stood behind the door and I willed her to disappear.

The forest's layers of fruits and branches begin their growth on the command of a clock. I had grown fuller also, to more potential, and scarcely knew I was sharpening for the spring's months.

I thrashed the letters around on the floor, kicking, scattering them. I sat on the floor and read the letters. The first was from Brother, a hello. Then two notes from a cousin, to whom I had written in the first place at Grandmother's urging; he lived in the region and had a thought disorder. He explained in his letter that he was now unemployed. The last part of his letter was lewd.

Grandmother was waiting.

"You told him to write this way to me," I accused.

She put two fingers of her left hand inside her mouth to say *yes*. A gesture she often used. Standing in the clearing, she held her cigarette in the sun.

My cousin's letter lingered in my mind and against my will I was warm. The prospect of an incompetent male causing my insides to jump up like saliva. It was Grandmother's doing.

"Seems like," Grandmother said, watching me, "you'd want to try him."

"*Bullshit, Grandmother*," I said. I hated knowing her. She had created a dilemma in which she would offer, then deny me, what she herself wanted, while provoking me so it was impossible for me to relate to her at all. I hated how, at first, I had solicited her with my puddly questions, my peon's search for reassurance. I had placated her. Now I had the pathogen-like belief that my anger would destroy us both.

I swept the floor clean and tightened the cabin door's hinges. The intruder was still approaching, always, getting closer. He was faceless in a white shirt. He would thump through the cedars, closer, tearing the ferns. When he burst from the forest and into the clearing, Grandmother would run to join him and I would scream.

The Fields

TO BEGIN WITH, we were far from the sea. My apartment door of soft aluminum never had the opportunity to hold back the sea.

My once-beautiful stepbrother had drowned, it seemed. There, standing on the porch, looking out: his new wife.

He stood next to her. The Fields were a family now, the ludicrous métier of which nearly drowned me too.

They were a complex family and they could not relax. The new wife ravened for more, wanted to be crammed with prosperity and more so each year; she sought to enthrall all comers with the velocity of her taste, her house, her son's forthcoming fame. Inexplicably, Stepbrother had married her.

They were very nearly wealthy. Their stomachs were sore. They drove through Illinois, Iowa, Kansas, expanding their businesses; they did not look back. They wanted all the candy of the world, the granite countertops, linen, vehicles, foreign maids. They wanted piano lessons and horses without having to take care of horses, boats and European spices and brand-name sexual climaxes and all other people must be surpassed; this was the Field family way, and they never stopped.

It was an odd time in my life. Night, the arena for sleep, occurred with startling frequency: every few hours. When I woke, a beetlike scent hung in the air like a pheromone; between coughs I flattened my joints in the sheets, imagining all manner of sufferings.

Stepbrother was now lost to me. Whereas once he had been a humid, fascinating being capable of comparing insect sex to the manufacture of silver, he was now merely a snob. His luminous half-precepts and lovely skin: disappeared. The new wife removed the flux from his eyes and the frequency of his gaze grew feeble. From my state of buried sexual loss I emerged gaudy and cross, wearing moss-covered sandals, slogging through sand.

Not long before, he and I had consoled one another frequently at sunrise. In a half-finished basement at sea level we practiced kung fu together in resolute silence.

In the first season of their marriage the rain made me stoic but I believed the wife had altered Stepbrother's chemistry and turned his veins sclerotic and green. Without a doubt he had changed. Striding to his vehicle each morning, he waved at me fatuously, failing to see me fully in my apartment with its long corrugated kitchen and tiny window pasted with newsprint. Behind him rose his new three-story home, its innards hushed as velour, enveloping the soft multitudes of his error.

Before, in the sparkling mud of our neighborhood, he had flown to our hiding place with thin calcareous limbs and faced me exclusively. His words fragmented around my ears and intoxicated me insofar as they were chaste and tried to deny what we both knew. He repeated his refusal to follow our family's demands, and with his pendulous hair and gauzy palms he belonged almost nowhere.

Perhaps Stepbrother merely became who he really was. It is true that in fits of wealth-seeking ascension—the buying up of businesses, the acquisition of a caged finch—he changed; then he and his wife, together, changed even more. The ease with which he understood these changes revealed character traits that previously he had concealed. The sequelae of his treachery went far beyond his lies and sudden, egregious moustache. Perfunctorily, violently, Stepbrother had affixed himself to the world. My disturbance grew when I recalled how, in the sand, he and I had talked of pushing away the world, while bending to one another's gentleness.

His new desire to please others melded with a vile, bland sexuality, and he chose his new wife from weakness, I alone knew. At the wedding party neighbors and family had clamored to him, swaying vegetally as if suspended in an oily extract of social convention and indeed, in a sense, he had broken free. I watched this repugnant transformation. Yet the precise nature of his former beauty still exists, at once real and impossible.

His profile being the sidereal light I still saw. It was the second year of their marriage, and I watched the Fields always now. In the afternoon I stood at my table, working out cardboard puzzles, screaming at Father over the phone for his insolence, his inability to swallow medicine; puzzle pieces dropped from my hands. I looked up, seeing the Fields' drapeless picture window where the new wife was drinking down a heinous frothy white drink. It is true that my anger toward her was ancient and that I should have suppressed the temptation to follow the tradition of female rivalry. But such an inhibition would have been useless. Instead, I pursued a disgust for her that gave me dull satisfaction.

Certainly the new wife was a creature who had, for example in high school, cried in order to manipulate her teachers, and she deserved my continued derision because she had not really changed. Now she starved herself most of the time, emitting an odor of wet cement and rapacity.

She had no sense of the strange, harlotish mystery of him.

Certainly I was a creature who could not feel pulses of love, at least not in the way others did. Admittedly instead I barred all people, though the act of predation held a purity for me that was piercing. Thus I found myself recalling Stepbrother's hydrated scent and hummocky arms, the way he had looked at me as if disregarding himself, and his summer shorts, a grindingly beautiful shade of blue. His silty averted eyes.

I had no intention of changing, and my exhaustion grew. In the summer of the second year I virtually destroyed my apartment in search of a cup of tepid tea. Across the length of the afternoon, I prepared a thick, blindingly white soup that was calming, though in the window I saw that the new wife had purchased several tiny sun dresses, and this addled me.

Through the window that spring I stared at her and at her child, too, who was now almost grown, his body sleek as a capsule and containing a quiet air of entitlement. The boy chewed languorously on a drinking straw. In a few moments the child sauntered outside to his new car and tore away, heading directly into the world to drink down its bylaws and customs as if they were distinctly unpoison. Sliding my hands, I cleared my table, unwell at the thought of the forthcoming family gathering. It would be a celebration; the Fields had made a business breakthrough.

On that day, Father appears in a wrinkled suit, beckoning. Voices of relatives mingle in a chord that tightens above the table loaded with glinting, unguent-like pates that absorb the heat of the sun. Unable to eat even vegetable matter, I note among the little aunts and female cousins a tall galutish one who, in fits of abnegation, tears herself from the group nucleus and stands at the rear of the yard below the high tension wires in anger: this is myself.

Stepbrother stands a few paces off in his aviator glasses and cheap muslinoid pants, holding, absurdly, a towel. Stepping close, I begin joking; he gives a friendly shove. I return the shove and so on. Further shoves arise, mock slaps to the neck, his neck, his immense eyelashes, drum-like temple; I take his fingers and vibrate them wildly as he ducks, feigning helplessness. But we both know that the sources of Stepbrother's power are, one, his abrupt change of personality; and two, the fact that he has taken root in the world. I watch him return to the patio, change into his swimming togs, my eye fixing upon the mottled striae of his hips which reveal, pleasingly, that he has gained weight. Father, standing by, pulls an insider's smile at Stepbrother, who, undeniably, has always been the favorite.

I approach, then lean back to kick Stepbrother's massive pelt; I tumble into him with my temper, pour jets of slaps and shoves over his naked trunk and legs, my throat straining as ladies look askance, trying to shield the eyes of their children as I suddenly yell, still glancing at the striae, "I AM COMING" while Stepbrother's laugh becomes complex as a howl—

The family sways back. We wait. The sea at three miles away is a kind of a clock, a liquid timepiece waiting paternally in order to assert its power to drown us.

Silence. The family ignores everything. The party resumes.

I begin another soft blow to Stepbrother's jaw, then stop: my useless excitement over him is gone.

The act of choosing a life is sad and requires that the discarded alternate lives atrophy in dirt and become hated.

Now, in the yard, a mild game of horseshoes is underway. The coming winter will be prosperous and full of family events. The businesses will expand; outside futures will rise, and the Fields, with their dark, curvaceous hair styles and hardy teeth, will be successful, strong, and safe.

Pressing a ham steak expertly to my mouth, I watch the family. Father shakes a handkerchief, jokes about football and wine; my moist-snouted cousins discuss property law.

My Stepbrother always knew there was nowhere else to go but here.

The swallowing of medicine is astonishingly unbitter.

The entire space of creation allows for happinesses of outsized proportions. Such is the joy of a fly who, streaking toward a lighted, open window, passes through effortlessly, without deliberation, into a territory of all.

This vast territory of the world gives countless children the opportunity to be born, to grow, to be cowed.

An ailanthus grows in a pot on the patio, and the pliant squeak of its leaves is tonic to me. The Fields' son drives up in his tony car, smiling cheeks swelled with good nutrition. The family's movements rise and fade in the manner of a dance. Previously I could not discern between values such as aberrance and strength, calamity and joy, insurrection and love; but now I have improved, fragrant with the succulence of hor d'oeuvres and dinner food. Who would ever intrude upon the Fields and their home? Despite my former troubles, despite all, I possess the active, glad heart of an outstanding relative, and looking to the Fields, I salute them.

Tippy Flowery

1

IF THERE WERE a sickmakingly tall person ever, it was she. She was all about sitting in her living room all day, all June, breathing billowishly, drinking tea from a membranously thin cup. One dim hallway led to an alley; another hall led out; my hair was brutishly cut; sitting opposite her and talking seemed equivalent, in effect, to being real.

For she was far too real, and I allowed this fact to soften my borders relentlessly. Her legs were crossed; her inhalations pulled as if weary soldiers; her expirations were scented of the flowers of tea. Outside the window, a deep gouge ran through sodless earth. A theatre of lilting puppets and geometric models hung from her living room ceiling, which was high, tall, made conical as if by her machines, the grip of her tight musculature.

Continuously I sought the key to the house bicycle, a long-boned, insect-like instrument that surely, at my command, would fly. Yet she knew where the key was kept, not I.

With her majestic moods and discontent, she was horridly real. I crept to the upstairs rooms of the house, stacking paper straws senselessly in an effort to remake this house, this town and month; I shaped the straws into an anvil-like ledge, hearing the faint squeak of leather masks, drips of urine, sex. She repeated a word again and again to my liking. At all peripheries: the sensation of pungent verdigris, school riots, and an adolescent purity of emotion that could not be maintained in daily life. An hour trailed past; I woke, pilfering a glance downstairs, turning to the scabby wall.

On the first floor, I could not find her anywhere. Do not worry, the house's calm, echoic rooms seemed to say: she will be back. She is gone momentarily due to a strong urge, each day, to launder her clothing.

2

Like an Argonaut, she wore smooth golden boots for exploring and I found in her wily smile a suggestion that the boots were correlated to, illustrative of, her intelligence. She was a fabulist, but only in the context of her house. Her fingers with their spatulate tips—flatter than any other part of her—appeared irregular, distorted. Objects from her bookshelves periodically dropped: sheaves of pamphlets, broken woodwind instruments, outsized plastic beetles, chipped butter plates, kite tails of vellum. I did not care for these objects. Again, I asked for the bicycle key. From one chemist to another, I tried to say, just between scientists, we, just between high-strung note-takers of this culture; but she just sat there, speaking mildly of corn futures, while the tea in her cup cooled, then warmed.

One morning she brandished a hair dryer, then dropped it into a pitcher of lemonade. She could get wild like that. In the microwave hunkered a pair of sneakers. I worried about the mucilaginous, slowly boiling water on the stove, about the exit slide off the bedroom window upstairs. Later, when the afternoon sky was hot and tallowish, she waited on the hard chair, her eyes scanning the surface of the mahogany tea, and at last she hinted at the bicycle key, offering details, for example: "It looks like a cookie."

3

She was utterly tall and kernel-sharp. Overall, though, she most bore a likeness to those types of hermitic music-collector men who rent darkish houses in the Midwest. Drinking magnificent amounts of the copper-colored tea, which carried in its astringency the vibration of music, dipping her finger into a salt dish, she sat while I attempted to derealize her, and failed. Her hands, small waterfalls, moved with a self-possession that, cruelly, did not require me at all. She was real and perspired tea; real, she labored hard at our nighttime endeavors; real, she stood a moment on the stairs, her arms now running with cooking oil; oily, she removed her headphones, sunglasses; I saw a tremendous province of empathy and willingness in her eyes—too messy. The key had been in a clay cup on the stairs all along. I filched it and ran for the bike.

It is all right to ride without a helmet. They do this in Europe everywhere. The pavement nearly glows when the ride is fast and smooth. I sped away from her house, with its dim, soft, worn gloves of rooms, the phalanges of all her apparatuses and belongings, the mean household gorgeousness altogether—worn books and the dry, dusty remains of cat food. It is well known among bicyclists that the present moment is too bright and diagonal, too floppy, too true.

How Do Breasts Feel?

How do breasts feel? How do they feel insofar as they are attached, insofar as you are with, behind them? When you cannot say "breasts" anymore because the word is too strong (English still contains the power to make its speakers squirm), and because of the difficulty in believing there are actually two of them, stop saying that word. Many people do not say it nationwide. Say "benches" instead, the easier way to put it, and easiest is best here in this place where we have no guides, seers, or helpers usually in our struggles.

Say "benches" while watching the body's scantest movements in night-private; say it while cupping a gray telephone, like a smallish baby, against your face; repeat the word—many do—while traveling across the bridge to sleep. You will know when you have arrived, for sleep is thin, yet inside it, our actions are balder, truer, more precise than ever possible during wakefulness.

Words may stir the body in public. Guard against this. Do not say "sac," with its animal candor, in the will call line, or "luscious" on voting day. Instead, say "stamp," "pavement," or "closure." Return home after voting, and sit on a hard, straight chair. Do not read books. Do not consider the patchy future. Avoid speaking to neighbors, and do not let them know your thoughts, especially not Mark and Carol Rush.

Say "benches" instead, or "wrists"; say these habitually, or in a pinch. No one will notice the discrepancy in meaning in any case. After voting day, hope for the best. Squeeze the words through your teeth. Hold the wrists still; do not allow them to fly free. As legions of words float skyward, try to hold them back. Instead of "wishing," say "ground." Taste nothing new such as an extended, wet, warm tongue, scantly sweet enough to make your eyes blink tears; do not bend your head. Do not lie down. Do not say "fathoms" or "salt," but "implication" and "united." Do not hold a word for too long.

Use no Spanish, with its vegetal, susurrating words, or French, with its emulsions of sentences. Speak in sharp, delimiting Anglo words instead: John does, Sarah does.

All neighbors stand in their living rooms, leaning calmly on mantels after voting day, for that is most reasonable. Protective of their inviolate, touched, half-permeated bodies, those fragrant, expressive objects for which at times the only thing to do is elicit more of the same: children. We guard our bodies, especially on the evening after voting day, and are careful with words. The bodies being the whole of what we have, save for our ability to make distance from others. Yet we also have furniture.

It is easy to supplant one word with another. It is so easy to taste one or the other.

Where do breasts begin? At which moments are they most important and satisfying, best? How to leave them open to bare rain? At which moments have you held yourself away, and how are you ambivalent?

Resting, pulling, breathing, smothering. Lying atop your wrists warmly on blankets through the fullness of an hour while the mind's sensations brim. The muscles move strongly in the back. We curve words into the empty places we know; we admit words to make them real. This will suffice. In between the minutes, consider the words yet to arrive. Do not mind the twinkling sensations, the music—that happens sometimes. For words rise, blur away, and then return, such important parts of your body.

174

Ears

Naturally this man was the most sensitive part of society, the tip, edge, the peninsula that wants so badly to thaw. For a long time, when he had been a female, he had shown off his body and its beauty in public, at all manner of parties, which now caused him, thinking of it, to feel tired. It had taken so many years for him to come into himself that he had no real home.

Now that he had made the change, his body took enormously new, different routes in order to function. It had been a cacophony, and the body had hurt; at last it had ceased hurting, or else had become strong enough to outpower its hurts. Now Brigg just wanted to stow his body away somewhere, far within a private den or simply inside eternity, so as to learn at last what nature really was, with its tireless hybridity.

But he was so excited about his new life that he couldn't focus or manage to earn a wage, so he went to live at his mother's house because she had not yet retired.

He had a few friends and phoned them sometimes to chat. He rested, waiting for his body to strengthen and push out something like a caul to protect him so he would be fine. Inside the refurbished porch/TV room he lay still, collecting warmth and, he imagined, a low, green fur that would coat him nourishingly with its bready aroma because his skin was so sweet and new.

He now wore short, rough, dark hair and a pen line beard along the jaw. As he rested on the couch, the mother sat close by and tended the parts of him they both acknowledged could remain baby-like—a complicity between them.

He looked at her with sleepy eyes.

I still know you, she said a little defensively.

She stayed at his side so protractedly, it seemed, as a way to care for herself. As she held him, Brigg grew back toward her, younger, because—it did not matter who he was—she was his mother. But when he whimpered about wanting a glass of water, she rolled her eyes and grinned at his regression.

He rested in snatches and his thin body grew toward the sun. Under a moppy purple shawl, he slept the type of light, cogent sleep rife with the pleasure it gives to the neck and back. Then he went deeper, dreaming of glassy lakes with rock islands, of a cat telling him the foods it liked—soft dreams that were gifts to himself, for they soothed and debrided the parts of him that were still raw.

Long ago in school, when he had been such a different person, the woodshop teacher, smoking outside the exit door, had said: Life is a difficult art.

Brigg could reproduce the teacher's voice inside his own ears if he wanted, the teacher's short laugh as if blowing a moment atop the neck of a bottle, for Brigg had always, his whole life, heard eerie things, like fingers stirring gravel, or cabbage leaves squeaking in the ground as he brushed by. Abruptly, he had heard the twang of the elastic string on a mask the night before during an argument with his brother, in which the brother's chief point was that he, Brigg, did not have a personality at all.

Brigg told the brother he did have a personality.

Not if you're a sexual vegetable, you don't, the younger brother said.

Don't be like this, Brigg begged. He was in his pajamas, his face sweating because the moment to talk about this with his brother had arrived so precipitously.

You took my sister and gave me a damn brother? That is not even in your power.

The brother was in his pajama bottoms, too, shirtless.

Brigg looked at his waist. I don't want anyone to feel bad about my life, he said.

Well, you're basically part of the weirdest category of people, the brother said, suddenly breaking into laughter as he heard himself say the words. Then, somehow, the siblings were close again and began a nervous mock-fight near the window without true punching, but instead with fists glancing, like they always had done, and then the brother was hugging onto Brigg with bluish alarm in his face, his eyes small and dark as a parakeet's. He pulled Brigg into a weak head lock; he was small-bodied and still only a student. Wriggling for a moment, Brigg's eyes teared and he enjoyed the soft comfort of the little brother's skin.

The brother shoved Brigg away and with a lost, hoarse voice said: I don't know what this world is about.

That was yesterday. Today the mother was working the long shift and had not yet come home. Brigg slept through the afternoon, and then, after waking, stood at the mirror behind the bedroom door, trying to acclimate to himself and to the day, despite the usual sensation of unreality.

He knew the little brother had probably just awakened, too, down the hall. Brigg gazed a few moments at his underwear, then dressed and moved toward the innermost rooms of the house. The yellow street light shellacked the gray porch stairs outside, and they looked more complete that way, as if the stairs had wanted the yellow light badly and waited all day for it.

The brother, sitting on his bed, gave a wave. Still sleepy, he asked Brigg not to go to the post office, since in their family, even small separations signified death.

The brother told Brigg he had heard something like kooks outside screaming in the night. Both the brothers heard things. The brother heard the crushing of weeds that meant someone was walking close, the sounds themselves manufacturing a story. Sometimes, when younger, he had yelped in the bathroom while the faucet was on, because he thought he heard voices in the running water.

They ate together; they sat on kitchen chairs and came to discuss sounds and ears. The brothers agreed they did not like that ears were always open and could not be shut like a mouth or an eye.

Maybe people's ears will change, said the brother. Down the line a thousand years. Medicine is amazing, he added, as if trying to reach Brigg. Someday, he said, doctors might invent a new kind of ears, more like attachments, soft fake ears. You could switch them off if you didn't feel like hearing.

Someday—why not? Brigg said, taking his coat, not paying much attention now.

I'd buy a pair, said the brother.

Brigg ignored him, and went to the post office. It was late now, possibly the middle of the night. It was cool, and even in the building's vestibule, the air was dry and exciting as autumn. Brigg dropped his driver's license form in the box, then watched as a nightshift worker pulled a heavy floor waxing machine in long, straight lines. The floor-waxer man was not friendly. Amidst the ammonia scent of the cleanser and wax that ran in foaming strips on the floor, the man's head hung low. Off to the side, near the wall, a buffer stood upright with its large round brush. Brigg liked the floor-waxer instantly; he looked as if he did not waste smiles and was slow, depressed, like most of the men with whom Brigg felt best. He stared until the floor-waxer looked at him, and, as if uncomfortable in being watched, the man gestured to the vinyl bench. Brigg went there and sat, waiting, breathing in the vestibule's polished silence, recalling hospital floors where night's stillness holds a special kind of erotics.

The floor-waxer shut down his machine using two switches, and the men sat on the bench. Brigg could not begin to speak, for he had too much history to himself, his body: so much had happened. After some time the floor-waxer stood and pulled on his coat, removing odorous leather gloves from the pockets; Brigg did not want the man to leave; he wished he had something with which to retain him, such as cookies.

Brigg heard a girl's laugh, which came from inside him—the voice of his old self. It shimmered up through his throat as if a bubble. He had thought she was mostly gone; she had been ugly in so many ways, and difficult. He always hated the girl's hateful life, the most difficult of anyone's life at high school. She had been the one with two bodies, and sometimes neither was real; it had always been horrible finding friends and sex; she had had to pull down all manner of shades in her mind so her body would function at all, and everything bad was the girl's fault, no one else's, she who had disgusted him and who was inside him still. Brigg saw, unpleasantly, that he should say goodbye to her if he really wanted her to go away. Then he heard her again, the rounded sound of her warm, asking voice. He always had had so much energy with which to hate her, but now, hearing her, nearly smelling her old skin, he ached to his palms for the lost, ugly little thing, the stubborn wart of long years who never had anything good in life. Brigg would turn to the floor-waxer, pull the man down on the bench beside him again; he would ask the floor-waxer to acknowledge the little thing inside Brigg, even to pet her if possible, to kiss her on the cheek because she had to be kissed; he would make the floor-waxer stare at his own small eyes hard and harder to see her, the little heart-shattered thing he had killed, and he would make the floor-waxer cry because it was goodbye.

The Water

IF IT WERE merely water and unimportant, but it is water, all-important, more brilliant than clean.

If water could rage back at us in a future of silver clashes. But water is merely itself—its body, its delirium of cohesion, its obeisance to gravity, its life as the house of fish—so water will never blame, only the people do that: for example, Gale, who lived in Tallahassee; he owned a rural house; he hated writing his thoughts. He liked tea at nighttime with the trees hanging near the fence, when there might be a mood in the air. And smoke (all through the waxy future, we will not lose such nights). He called his wife "Mother"; he lived on a hill. Gale did not vote this time. He was not a bad man, not through all the bad years while Florida lost its lakes and he watched, while the lizards died papery in the grass. The lakes' deaths were a shame, Gale said, resting in his chair, and Mother wrote a blaming letter to a magazine. Gale liked chicken. His children would soon retire. The water will be algae-oily and never consciously suffer.

We might reach an arm toward a dark surface someday, gasping alongside the rowboats and birds, alongside this incomprehension of water and the way those living at the top always rule. Gale knew it. Still and all, he was glad he lived. He said to Mother, Hi, Koo-koo. Aren't you glad you lived too?

Stacey Levine is the author of *My Horse and Other Stories* (PEN/West Award) and the novels *Dra—* and *Frances Johnson* (Finalist, Washington State Book Award). A Pushcart Prize nominee and winner of the 2009 Stranger Literary Genius award, her fiction has appeared in the *Denver Quarterly, Fence, Tin House, The Fairy Tale Review, Seattle Magazine, The Santa Monica Review, Yeti,* and many other venues. She has also contributed to *American Book Review, Bookforum, The Stranger, The Chicago Reader, The Seattle Times,* and *The Seattle Post-Intelligencer.*

Also available from Starcherone Books

Kenneth Bernard, *The Man in the Stretcher: previously uncollected stories*
Donald Breckenridge, *You Are Here*
Blake Butler and Lily Hoang, eds., *Thirty Under Thirty: An Anthology of Innovative Fiction by Younger Writers*
Joshua Cohen, *A Heaven of Others*
Peter Conners, ed., *PP/FF: An Anthology*
Jeffrey DeShell, *Peter: An (A)Historical Romance*
Nicolette deCsipkay, *Black Umbrella Stories*, illustrated by Francesca deCsipkay
Raymond Federman, *My Body in Nine Parts*, with photographs by Steve Murez
Raymond Federman, *Shhh: The Story of a Childhood*
Raymond Federman, *The Voice in the Closet*
Raymond Federman and George Chambers, *The Twilight of the Bums*, with cartoon accompaniment by T. Motley
Sara Greenslit, *The Blue of Her Body*
Johannes Göransson, *Dear Ra: A Story in Flinches*
Joshua Harmon, *Quinnehtukqut*
Harold Jaffe, *Beyond the Techno-Cave: A Guerrilla Writer's Guide to Post-Millennial Culture*
Janet Mitchell, *The Creepy Girl and other stories*
Alissa Nutting, *Unclean Jobs for Women and Girls*
Aimee Parkison, *Woman with Dark Horses: Stories*
Ted Pelton, *Endorsed by Jack Chapeau 2 an even greater extent*
Thaddeus Rutkowski, *Haywire*
Leslie Scalapino, *Floats Horse-Floats or Horse-Flows*
Nina Shope, *Hangings: Three Novellas*

Purchase through www.starcherone.com, from your favorite bookseller, or through Starcherone Books, PO Box 303, Buffalo, NY 14201

Starcherone Books, Inc., is a 501(c)(3) non-profit whose mission is to stimulate public interest in works of innovative fiction. In addition to encouraging the growth of amateur and professional authors and their audiences, Starcherone seeks to educate the public in self-publishing and encourage the growth of other small presses. Visit us online at www.starcherone.com.

We are a signatory to the Book Industry Treatise on Responsible Paper Use and use postconsumer recycled fiber paper in our books.

Starcherone Books is an independently operated imprint of Dzanc Books.